T0012904

Cryptid Creatures

CRYPTID CREATURES
A Field Guide

Kelly Milner Halls

Illustrated by
Rick Spears

little bigfoot
an imprint of sasquatch books
seattle, wa

Copyright © 2019 by Kelly Milner Halls
Illustrations copyright © 2019 by Rick Spears

All rights reserved. No portion of this book may be reproduced or utilized in any form, or by any electronic, mechanical, or other means, without the prior written permission of the publisher.

Manufactured in China by C&C Offset Printing Co. Ltd. Shenzhen, Guangdong Province, in March 2023

LITTLE BIGFOOT with colophon is a registered trademark of Penguin Random House LLC

27 26 25 24 23   10 9 8 7 6 5 4

Editor: Christy Cox and Ben Clanton | Production editor: Jill Saginario | Design: Tony Ong

Library of Congress Cataloging-in-Publication Data
Names: Halls, Kelly Milner, 1957- author. | Spears, Rick, illustrator.
Title: Cryptid creatures : a field guide / Kelly Milner Halls ;
    illustrated by Rick C. Spears.
Description: Seattle : Sasquatch Books, [2019] | Includes index. |
    Audience: Age 7. | Audience: Grade 4 to 6.
Identifiers: LCCN 2019003129 | ISBN 9781632172105 (trade paperback)
Subjects: LCSH: Monsters--Identification--Juvenile literature. |
    Cryptozoology--Juvenile literature. | Animals--Folklore--
    Juvenile literature.
Classification: LCC QL89 .H358 2019 | DDC 001.944--dc23
LC record available at https://lccn.loc.gov/2019003129

ISBN: 978-1-63217-210-5

Sasquatch Books
1325 Fourth Avenue, Suite 1025
Seattle, WA 98101
SasquatchBooks.com

To Thomas Dabler, Logan and Griffin Shaw,
Kevin Tsuchida, and Harrison Collins—five
boys who have inspired me as they've grown
into young men.

                                          —KMH

To my lovely bride, Darlene, who puts up with
all kinds of weird stuff . . . especially me.

                                          —RS

CONTENTS

Cryptid Extras

Appendices

INTRODUCTION

For hundreds of years, people have seen and documented animal life worldwide. Zoology is the study of confirmed animal species—creatures captured, studied, and verified as real by the scientific community. But what about animals seen but unconfirmed—animals that fall between the realms of real and imaginary on the scientific spectrum?

Cryptozoology is the study of those mysterious sightings. And this book is a close examination of fifty of those rare possibilities, arranged alphabetically and classified by types. It explores the best possible evidence available for each featured creature, including scientific papers, magazine and newspaper articles, and credible eyewitness accounts.

Will we prove that all of the creatures in this book are real? Not likely. Some have been confirmed as real. Some are absolutely fake. But most remain somewhere in between. As professional and amateur cryptozoologists work in the field to uncover the truth, the facts will come into sharper focus. But until they do, a closer look at what we know now will captivate our imaginations. So evaluate the evidence and use your critical-thinking skills to form an opinion. Then search for more evidence as you investigate the mysteries on your own.

Reality Ratings

Until definitive information is available, each cryptid will be given a "reality rating."

★   The cryptid has been confirmed as a hoax.

★★   Proof is not available, and it has yet to be confirmed as a hoax, but the odds are against the cryptid being real.

★★★   Some evidence supports the possibility of the cryptid being real.

★★★★   Evidence is fairly substantial that the stories of the cryptid might be true.

★★★★★   The cryptid may be confirmed as real in the not-so-distant future.

★★★★★★   The creature once known as a cryptid has been proven real.

Cryptid Creatures

*Adult Ahool resembles
a gigantic bat*

AHOOL

(ah-WHOL)

FIRST REPORTED:	1925
LOCATION:	JAVA, INDONESIA
CRYPTID TYPE:	AERIAL; BAT-LIKE
REALITY RATING:	★ ★ ★

FACTOID: Dr. Ernest Bartels is the naturalist who discovered this bat-like cryptid in 1925. After hearing it screech "ahool, ahool, ahool," he named it for its strange vocalization.

EYEWITNESS ACCOUNT: While naturalist Dr. Bartels is credited with spotting the black-and-gray Ahool in Indonesia, he is not the only person to make such a claim. In August of 2015, student Pedro Roque reported seeing a similar creature in Almada, Portugal, which is on the Tagus River.

"I and another friend heard a noise above," Pedro told the *Cryptozoology News*. "It looked like a large flying animal, perhaps a giant bat."

With a ten-foot wingspan and spearing teeth, the Ahool is thought to be a fish eater, and its proximity to a river supports that theory. Pedro and his friends tracked the animal for a few seconds before it disappeared into the thick brush.

An anonymous fifty-year-old minister and her daughter tracked a similar animal while bird-watching in the Stone Lakes National Wildlife Refuge south of Sacramento, California, in 1994.

For twenty minutes, what they called a pterodactyl-like creature circled the sky, leaving the two women stunned. They retreated to their car, where they continued talking about the sighting. The mother later spoke to the *Cryptozoology News*.

"I remember I said, 'That's impossible. They are an extinct species.' My daughter, who was well read on extinct birds, kept pointing out the unusual features of this animal," including a pterodactyl-like head with a pointed beak, and wings unlike those of a bird. "It had a large wingspan, bigger than a blue heron. It was gliding very high up, with very little flapping movement of its wings." "I didn't think I could call [the] Audubon Society and tell them about the sighting, because this bird was not on their checklist." She felt they would have likely told her that it was "a crane or a heron. Believing that would certainly solve things, but my brain wouldn't rest." She maintains that what they saw was a real living animal "straight out of Jurassic Park."

Adult Ahool skull

Juvenile Ahool or pup

Cryptozoologist Ivan Sanderson suspected the Ahool might be related to an African cryptid known as the Kongamato (see page 109), which also resembled a pterosaur, according to local witnesses.

Neither the giant bat nor the pterodactyl-like animal have been scientifically proven, but witnesses are adamant about what they've seen.

AKKOROKAMUI

(ack-oh-roc-ah-MU-ee)

FIRST REPORTED:	UNKNOWN
LOCATION:	HOKKAIDO, JAPAN
CRYPTID TYPE:	AQUATIC; OCTOPUS-LIKE
REALITY RATING:	★ ★ ★ ★

FACTOID: Shrines dedicated to Akkorokamui dot the Japanese landscape. Because the creature can amputate and regrow its tentacles, meditations at the shrines are thought to aid healing and spiritual turmoil.

EYEWITNESS ACCOUNT: For centuries, the indigenous Ainu people of Japan have passed down stories of the Akkorokamui from generation to generation. Said to lurk in Funka Bay off the island of Hokkaido, the enormous, twelve-tentacled red giant—more than a football field in length—is both feared and worshipped.

Is the octopus-like creature, similar to the Kraken (see page 112), a work of fiction or a factual being? It's hard to know. But its reputation for swallowing vessels whole forced

Akkorokamui may be related to the octopus

Newly hatched Akkorokamui

fishermen to sail through the bay at alert, sharp sickles in hand to battle Akkorokamui attacks should they be launched.

Nineteenth-century missionary John Batchelor recorded the ancient stories in his book, *The Ainu and Their Folklore.*

"Three men," he wrote, "were out trying to catch a sword-fish, when all at once a great sea-monster, with large staring eyes, appeared in front of them and proceeded to attack the boat. A desperate fight ensued. The monster was round in shape, and emitted a dark fluid and noxious odour. The three men fled in dismay, not so much indeed for fear, they say, but on account of the dreadful smell."

Without further evidence, it's hard to be sure if Japan has a kraken-like cryptid or not. But with so much of the ocean left unexplored, mysteries are undoubtedly waiting to be fully discovered—perhaps even giant Japanese cephalopods.

*Detached Akkorokamui arms
could allegedly grow back*

Almasty may be Russia's Sasquatch

ALMASTY

(al-MAST-ee)

FIRST REPORTED:	**1850s**
LOCATION:	**ABKHAZIA**
CRYPTID TYPE:	**TERRESTRIAL; HUMANOID-LIKE**
REALITY RATING:	★ ★ ★ ★ ★

FACTOID: Russian people in what is now known as Abkhazia claimed to have captured one female Almasty ("wild man or woman") in the 1850s. They tamed the six-foot-six-inch tall female and named her Zana. She later mated with humans to produce several children, including a son named Khwit. DNA testing on Khwit suggested the creatures were modern humans, but believers, including Professor Bryan Sykes of the University of Oxford, cling to the Neanderthal or prehistoric human theory. DNA testing on Zana's living descendants show Zana's ancestors were African.

EYEWITNESS ACCOUNT: Nineteenth-century Russians may have been the first to witness the Almasty, but Russian journalist and eyewitness Nina Grinyova claims to have come face to face with a "wild man" a century later. While strolling through the mountain wilderness in 1980, an eighteen-year-old Nina heard the male Almasty as he clacked two stones together.

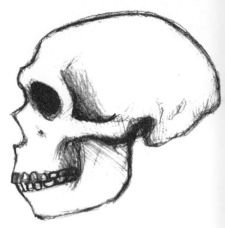

Could Almasty be a Neanderthal (skull pictured here)?

Unafraid, she walked toward him. Hoping to entertain the creature, she pulled a toy rubber duck from her coat pocket. The squeaky sound frightened the mystery man, who turned and ran. But Nina never forgot her encounter.

British cryptozoologist Adam Davies believed the journalist, and he continues the search for the Almasty in China's Mongolian steppes, a second location known for the creature. Both Nina and Adam tell their stories in a *National Geographic* documentary, "Russian Bigfoot."

A young Almasty learning to survive

ALTAMAHA-HA

(al-tah-mah-HA-ha)

FIRST REPORTED:	**1969**
LOCATION:	**GEORGIA, UNITED STATES**
CRYPTID TYPE:	**AQUATIC; RIVER MONSTER-LIKE**
REALITY RATING:	★ ★ ★ ★

FACTOID: A life-size model of a juvenile Altamaha-ha, also known as "Altie," is on display in the Rock Eagle Natural History Museum in Eatonton, Georgia. Another is exhibited at the Darien-McIntosh Visitor Center in Darien, Georgia.

EYEWITNESS ACCOUNT: Indigenous people told stories of a giant river monster long before recorded history. But dozens of people have shared stories in the centuries since, including Benny Coursey, a Georgia fisherman.

Benny Coursey wasn't headed for church on the Sunday he met a mysterious creature. According to the *Augusta Chronicle*, he and a friend were out to catch a few fish near Baxley, Georgia, on the Altamaha River. They didn't catch a thing, but they did see something amazing.

Altamaha-ha, fully grown

"It looked like a big snake, a real whopper, with its head reared out of the water," Coursey said in the article. But that wasn't the end of it. The massive creature—roughly twenty feet long—came right at his favorite boat "like it meant business."

The gunmetal-colored animal picked up speed, undulating with an up-and-down motion like a dolphin, not side-to-side like a fish. The wake it stirred up confirmed it was picking up speed. Coursey and his friend braced for impact, expecting the wooden boat to splinter. But the creature suddenly dove under water, then reappeared on the other side of the boat.

The two men sat white-faced and confused as the creature disappeared down the river. Had the legendary Altamaha-ha spared them? Coursey was never sure. "The good Lord was with us," he said.

Coursey isn't the only eyewitness. In 1998, three young men also saw Altie.

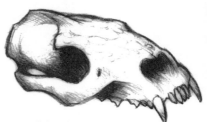

Adult Altamaha-ha skull

Rusty Davis, Bennett Bacon, and Owen Lynch were about thirteen years old when they headed for the Eulonia community dock near Bennett's grandparents' home in Georgia. It was a steamy day in May and they wanted to cool down.

Bennett was the first to jump into the river, as his two friends watched from the dock. "It came up ten feet from him," Rusty said in a newspaper account. "We were screaming at him to get out of the water."

He knew his friends were serious when he turned to see a large, blue-gray tail surface beside him. Bennett never swam as fast as he did that afternoon. He even scraped his belly on the dock as he rushed to escape the danger. "Yeah, I was scared," he said. Who wouldn't be?

Experts believe the sightings are a matter of misidentification. Altie might be a sturgeon or a manatee, not a sea monster. And physical proof has been scarce. But one recent sighting came close.

According to *National Geographic*, the decomposing remains of a strange creature washed ashore in March of 2018 at the Wolf Island National Wildlife Refuge near Darien, Georgia. Witness Jeff Warren thought the foul-smelling carcass was a seal at first. But as he got closer, something else came to mind.

"It looked more like a baby sea monster or a throwback to the Jurassic," according to the *Savannah Morning News*. Warren quickly took a few photos on his cell phone and sent them to local media outlets. Was this proof of the Altamaha-ha?

Local experts were doubtful. "It looks like a deep-sea shark, like a frilled shark," said Chantal Audran of the Tybee Island Marine Science Center. But without examining the body in person, she said she couldn't be sure.

Naturalist John Crawford, a marine educator at University of Georgia Marine Extension, considers it a hoax, a model made of clay. "Whoever did it did a good job," he said.

Closer study could confirm which theory is true. But the body disappeared almost as quickly as it appeared. Was it gathered up by the person who launched the hoax? Or did the body of an Altamaha-ha slip back into a watery grave? We may never know.

Altie pup

The so-called African unicorn was an okapi

A'NASA

(an-AH-sah)

FIRST REPORTED:	1847
LOCATION:	KORDOFAN, SUDAN
CRYPTID TYPE:	TERRESTRIAL; GIRAFFE-LIKE
REALITY RATING:	★ ★ ★ ★ ★ ★

FACTOID: The A'nasa is also called the African unicorn, or okapi. According to Dr. Noelle Kumpel of Zoological Society of London's Conservation Policy Programme, the okapi are "very shy and rare animals," which is why scat and other trace evidence are often the only indications the creature has not fallen into extinction.

Adult A'nasa skull

EYEWITNESS ACCOUNT: According to the legends, scientist Baron Johann Wilhelm von Müller joined an African animal expedition in 1847. As he questioned residents about local wildlife, he began to hear stories of an African unicorn called A'nasa.

The first man von Müller spoke to said the A'nasa was about the size of a small donkey and had a single horn on its head. When the animal was calm, the horn was limp against its forehead. But when danger approached, the horn grew stiff as a defensive weapon.

The animal was said to have brittle bones and was hunted for its skin. Used to cover shields, the skin allegedly fortified the protective instruments.

Weeks later, von Müller met a second man who told a similar story, with a twist. Not only had the man seen the A'nasa, he'd eaten it. According to the witness, it was delicious.

In 2008, the British newspaper the *Daily Mail* proclaimed that photographic evidence for the African unicorn had been captured in the jungle of the Democratic Republic of the Congo. The animal often called a unicorn turned out to be the elusive okapi. This distant cousin of the giraffe has a tiny bump on its head, resembling a tiny horn.

It was captured on film, thanks to a series of camera traps set up by the Zoological Society of London and the Congolese Institute for Nature Conservation.

A'nasa babies were related to giraffes

BEAST OF BUSCO

(beast of BUS-coe)

FIRST REPORTED:	**1898**
LOCATION:	**INDIANA, UNITED STATES**
CRYPTID TYPE:	**AQUATIC/ TERRESTRIAL; TURTLE-LIKE**
REALITY RATING:	★ ★ ★ ★

FACTOID: The Beast of Busco, also known as Oscar, is so important to Churubusco, Indiana, that they celebrate it once a year with "Turtle Days." For almost seventy years, they've held an annual parade, raffles, fireworks, and more—all to honor the giant snapping turtle that got away.

EYEWITNESS ACCOUNT: Farmer Oscar Fulk saw it first in 1898—an enormous snapping turtle with a shell the size of a compact car and a head the size of a child. He swore it swam in the seven-acre lake near his homestead, but no one believed him.

Fifty years later, Ora Blue and Charley Wilson saw the five-hundred-pound monster turtle while fishing the same lake, now known as Fulk Lake. Word spread, thanks

This giant snapping turtle could feed on deer

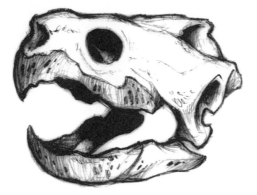

Adult Beast of Busco skull

to a story on the newspaper wire service, and the surge for sightings was on.

Mobs of people rushed to Fulk Lake to catch a glimpse of the beast, nicknamed "Oscar," a legendary turtle that could bite off the arm of a strong man with ease—in theory. But it didn't reveal itself.

When the public questioned the authenticity of the story, landowner Gale Harris tried to drain the lake to prove Oscar was real. But the search was unsuccessful. A year later, a deep-sea diver set out to solve the mystery, but brought the wrong equipment. Even *Life* magazine set out to document Oscar in photographs, but failed.

Turtles hatch from leathery eggs

The Beast of Busco was never seen again, but its legend may live forever.

Cartoon Cryptids

Cartoonist Jay Stephens launched *The Secret Saturdays* in 2008. The Saturday family searched for cryptids, aiming to protect not only their fellow humans but the vulnerable animals as well. The TV show celebrated cryptids, but it wasn't the first cartoon feature to do so.

In 1932, Disney introduced mermaids in *King Neptune*. *Peter Pan* revived Disney's cartoon mermaids in 1953. Warner Brothers created *Beany and Cecil*, a show about a boy and his sea monster, in 1959.

Daffy Duck led the Abominable Snowman to Bugs Bunny in 1961. Goofy met Bigfoot in *A Goofy Movie* in 1995. And the New Looney Tunes matched Bugs with a recurring Bigfoot friend in 2015.

The Scooby-Doo crew searched for the ghost of Bigfoot in 1972. *Scooby-Doo and the Loch Ness Monster* debuted as a feature-length film in 2004.

Homer Simpson of *The Simpsons* was mistaken for Bigfoot in 1990. Mr. Burns tried to bring the Loch Ness Monster to Springfield in 1999. Casper the Ghost met Bigfoot in 1995.

Monster High debuted in 2010 and featured many creatures of cryptozoology. And the *Ducktales* reboot featured Bigfoot in 2018.

The list is far from complete, but like all cryptids, if you keep searching, you may make new cartoon cryptid discoveries of your own.

Sasquatch, nicknamed "Bigfoot," may raid the food stores of campers

BIGFOOT

(BIG-foot)

FIRST REPORTED:	**1958**
LOCATION:	**CALIFORNIA, UNITED STATES**
CRYPTID TYPE:	**TERRESTRIAL; APE-LIKE**
REALITY RATING:	★ ★ ★ ★ ★

FACTOID: An exact replica of the Ray Wallace wooden Bigfoot "shoes" are on display at the International Cryptozoology Museum in Portland, Maine, thanks to Loren Coleman's thoughtful curation.

EYEWITNESS ACCOUNT: For decades, if not centuries, the people native to Bluff Creek, California, told stories of a giant, hair-covered creature wandering the rugged trails of their tree-covered wilderness—stealing the food of local Hoopa tribal members, wrecking mining equipment, and tossing giant stones as if they were baseballs.

Native people seldom questioned the stories, but those without such ancient roots were skeptics—until the fall of 1958.

National Park Service road construction crews employed by Ray Wallace began to notice sixteen-inch footprints in the mud of their workplace. Not one track, not two, but dozens cascaded down steep hillsides, across the emerging roads, around bulldozers, and back up the hills. After seeing the tracks for several days, workman and eyewitness Jerry Crew brought plaster of paris to capture reverse copies of the tracks as evidence.

Adult Bigfoot skull

Reporters at the *Humbolt Times* in nearby Eureka, California, saw the plaster casts and began to write about the mysterious visitor. To their amazement, the stories spread across the United States. The creature had been called many names before 1958, but the newspapers nicknamed it "Bigfoot" in honor of the size of the tracks.

When foreman Ray Wallace died in 2002, his children made a bold claim. Their father had created Bigfoot as an elaborate prank. They produced a pair of carved, wooden feet as proof. Newspapers proclaimed the death of a legend from Los Angeles to New York City. Many thought the rumors had been put to rest. Others expressed doubt. There were footprints put down by the wooden feet, but Jerry Crew's plaster casts were not made by Wallace's wooden feet. And other plaster casts collected by other witnesses had their own distinctive characteristics.

When Roger Patterson and Bob Gimlin captured one minute and six seconds of film of what they said was the creature in October of 1967—near Bluff Creek, California—the 1958 debate resurfaced with a vengeance, and it continues today.

"Bigfoot" was never the actual name for this creature. It is a physical description of the muddy tracks, little more than a nickname. Similar creatures known by other names (Sasquatch, Skunk Ape, Yowie, and more—see the partial list on page 202) have been reported on almost every continent around the world.

Baby Bigfoot would depend on its mother for years

BURU

(BUH-rue)

FIRST REPORTED:	1944
LOCATION:	HIMALAYAS, INDIA
CRYPTID TYPE:	TERRESTRIAL/ AQUATIC; LIZARD-LIKE
REALITY RATING:	★ ★ ★ ★ ★

FACTOID: Apa Tani villagers of India said the Buru was a large, exotic lizard. Its twenty-inch-long head featured a flattened snout, a forked tongue, and two pairs of pointed teeth protruding out of the upper and lower jaws of the front of its mouth. Its elongated neck could raise its head above the water or retract it to be closer to the surface. The thick, scaleless body slipped through the water with ease. It preferred the deeper water but came to shore when the summer heat turned its lakes to shallows. Elusive and seldom seen, the Buru had a deep, bellowing cry that struck fear in the hearts of locals, even though it was considered a vegetarian and didn't even eat fish.

Buru may have been a lizard lost to extinction

EYEWITNESS ACCOUNT: Though anthropologist and Buru expert Christopher von Fürer-Haimendorf never actually saw the creature on his extensive travels to India, he interviewed dozens of local witnesses and came to believe the tales of a six- to ten-foot-long lizard with long, strong clawed legs. He shared his findings with zoologist Charles Stoner, who conducted a study of his own and published a scientific paper on his findings.

When the British newspaper the *Daily Mail* heard about the exotic Himalayan "dragon," they sponsored an expedition to find a living Buru. Famed adventurer, spy, war hero, and journalist Ralph Izzard was living in India at the time and enthusiastically joined the quest. Though the team never found a living specimen, additional eyewitness reports

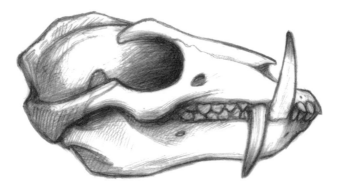

Adult Buru skull

Baby Buru

convinced Izzard the creature was real—so real, the journalist wrote a book about it—*The Hunt for the Buru*—in 1951.

Izzard's reputation as a rugged man of the world was said to be the inspiration for Sir Ian Fleming's fictional literary character, James Bond. Was the Buru as imaginary as Bond? It's hard to say. But most people now living in the Buru's alleged habitat believe the animal was driven extinct due to the Apa Tani villagers' purposeful slaughter.

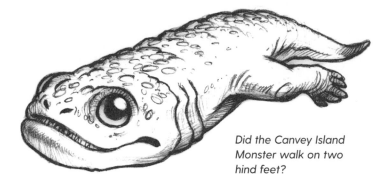

Did the Canvey Island Monster walk on two hind feet?

CANVEY ISLAND MONSTER

(CAN-vee Island Monster)

FIRST REPORTED:	1953
LOCATION:	ESSEX, ENGLAND
CRYPTID TYPE:	AQUATIC; FISH-LIKE
REALITY RATING:	★ ★

FACTOID: Illustrations of the Canvey Island Monster of Britain sometimes appear to be cute, bipedal creatures similar to the Murloc of the *World of Warcraft* video game—not counting Murloc's arms and head quills.

EYEWITNESS ACCOUNT: In November of 1953, something strange washed up on the shores of Canvey Island in the United Kingdom. Though some decomposition had set in thanks to the open air of dry land, the carcass appeared to have thick, brick-red skin, bulging eyes, and gills. While this

Canvey Island Monster may
be a frogfish (pictured here)

Babies probably
hatched from eggs

was not so unusual for an aquatic creature, there were more odd details.

Two hind legs with five-toed, curved feet and curved arches implied that the creature was a biped—it might have walked on those legs.

Experts could not identify the species of animal, but determined it posed no danger to the public and had it cremated. Nine months later, a second, larger specimen washed ashore. The second body was fresher, so scientists collected skin samples from the eyes, nostrils, and teeth.

Even with the tissue samples, the identity was still uncertain, and the second body vanished.

Some who examined photographs of the second body speculated that it might be an anglerfish whose fins had been mistaken for arched feet. Others thought it was a frogfish, a species that does walk on leg-like fins, has bulging eyes, and can be reddish brown in color.

Without a body to examine further, the Canvey Island Monster remains a mystery until the next strange, aquatic body makes its way to shore.

The Cardiff Giant, compared here to a man of average height, was a giant hoax

CARDIFF GIANT

(CAR-dif Giant)

FIRST REPORTED:	1869
LOCATION:	NEW YORK, UNITED STATES
CRYPTID TYPE:	TERRESTRIAL; HUMANOID-LIKE
REALITY RATING:	★

FACTOID: The Cardiff Giant, a huge stone statue of a man, was so popular in its day that several replicas were created, including one for famous sideshow promoter P. T. Barnum. Barnum passed his copy off as the original to draw more paying customers to his traveling displays of amazements and oddities.

EYEWITNESS ACCOUNT: After a heated debate with a revivalist minister in 1867, nonbeliever George Hull hatched a secret plan. If the Bible's book of Genesis claimed there were "giants in the earth," he would plant one to fool his religious neighbors.

Hull bought a five-ton slab of gypsum stone in Fort Dodge, Iowa, in 1868, telling the merchant it would be used for a statue of President Abraham Lincoln. He shipped the slab to Chicago, Illinois, where sculptor Edward Burghardt was commissioned to create a ten-foot statue of Hull, not Lincoln—and it was a naked statue.

Once complete, Hull shipped the sculpture to farmer William "Stub" Newell in Cardiff, New York. Newell promised to keep the scheme a secret in exchange for a piece of the profits, once the fake "giant" was found and displayed as a biblical miracle. They buried the giant and waited.

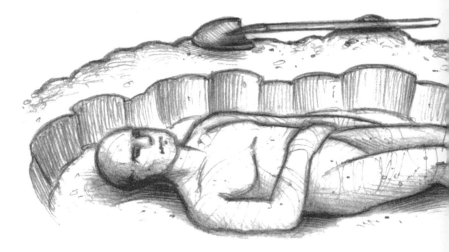

Once unearthed, the giant amazed

A year later, Hull told Newell to launch the hoax. The farmer hired two men to dig a well on the farm and showed them exactly where to dig—where he knew the statue was buried. When metal shovels met stone, a new "world wonder" was unearthed. Religious leaders believed it was an ancient giant petrified by God, turned from flesh to stone.

In time, scientists, including famed Yale paleontologist and dinosaur fossil collector Othniel Charles Marsh, confirmed the statue was a hoax very recently carved, but not before Hull and Newell had collected as much as $30,000 from curious visitors at fifty cents apiece. Though several copies were made, the original is on display at the Farmers' Museum in Cooperstown, New York.

Stone giants are carved, not born

CHAMP

(chAMP)

FIRST REPORTED:	1819
LOCATION:	VERMONT, UNITED STATES
CRYPTID TYPE:	AQUATIC; SEA MONSTER
REALITY RATING:	★ ★ ★ ★

FACTOID: In 1873, and again in 1887, famed showman P. T. Barnum offered a reward for the capture of Champ, the Lake Champlain sea monster. He offered $50,000 for the creature, dead or alive. Not a soul collected the hefty prize, which would have been worth almost $1 million today.

EYEWITNESS ACCOUNT: Before recorded history, the native Abenaki and Iroquois tribes of the region told stories of a ten-foot-long creature—now known as Champ—swimming the waters of Lake Champlain in New York and Vermont. More than three hundred people have claimed sightings. But none are more compelling than the late Sandra Mansi's photo-documented encounter.

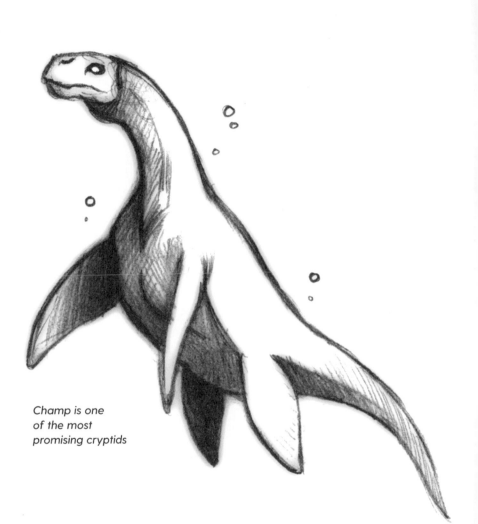

Champ is one
of the most
promising cryptids

On July 5, 1977, Sandra, her two children (Heidi, eleven, and Larry, twelve), and her then-fiancé (later husband) Anthony Mansi stopped by the lake near the Canadian border in Vermont. After a hike, the kids took off their shoes to wade in the lake. Anthony went back to the car to get Sandra's camera.

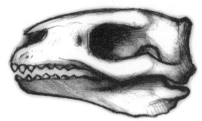

Adult Champ skull

As she watched her children play, Sandra saw movement about one hundred and fifty feet out. At first, she thought it was a school of fish. As the head and neck peeked out of the water, she thought it was a large sturgeon. But when that neck rose more than five feet out of the water, she knew it was no sturgeon.

Anthony knew it too as he reappeared, screaming for the kids to get out of the lake. He handed the camera to Sandra so he could help her up, but she didn't retreat. She snapped a picture and captured what *Discover* magazine called the "Rosetta Stone of Champology"—a semi-clear picture of a legend.

Sandra studied the creature for five full minutes. She estimated that it was between twelve and fifteen feet long. It lingered until the sound of a boat rang out in the near distance. Sandra saw its head turn, reacting to the motor, then saw it slip back into the depths of the lake.

As the family drove home they wondered, "What did we just see?" And Champ was their only conclusion. But what *is* Champ? Some say the creature resembles a *Basilosaurus*, an ancient whale that lived forty to thirty-four million years ago. Could a small colony of prehistoric whales have survived as freshwater mammals?

Scientist Elizabeth von Muggenthaler has collected evidence to support the possibility. In 2003, the animal sound expert conducted an audio survey of the lake. Most of the sounds matched animals known to inhabit Lake Champlain. But one remained a mystery. Something in the water was using echolocation, the way dolphins and whales do in the sea. A similar study in 2013 also claimed to capture echolocation, though it has not been confirmed.

Is a colony of whales living in Lake Champlain? Only time will tell. But thanks to binding legislation in New York and Vermont, all relatives of Champ have protected status. People hunting and fishing are not allowed to capture or kill the creature, should it surface within reach. And that's a good thing—just in case.

Baby Champ

Chupacabras were bipedal in early legends

CHUPACABRA

(chue-pah-CAH-bra)

FIRST REPORTED:	**1995**
LOCATION:	**PUERTO RICO, UNITED STATES**
CRYPTID TYPE:	**TERRESTRIAL; DOG-LIKE**
REALITY RATING:	★ ★ ★

FACTOID: Though dozens claim to have spotted four-legged Chupacabras in Texas and other Southwestern states during the past ten years, the animals have turned out to be of canine origin. They are dogs, coyotes, wolves, or hybrids with advanced illnesses, not the mysterious Chupacabras.

EYEWITNESS ACCOUNT: In 1995, Puerto Rican newspapers featured terrifying headlines about the Chupacabra, which in Spanish means "goat sucker." Dozens of goats, chickens, horses, and other livestock were apparently being drained of their blood. Two puncture marks at

Adult Chupacabra skull

the victims' throats suggested a hungry vampire was on a killing spree.

Eyewitness Madelyne Tolentino believes she saw the beast firsthand. She describes an animal that stood on two legs, had dark eyes, long gangly limbs, and spikes down its back. She swore it was real, but it was unlike any animal ever previously described in real life. In Tolentino's region, it was called *El Vampiro de Moca*. But the name "Chupacabra" later took root.

Stories of blood-drained livestock sprung up all over Puerto Rico, then spread to Mexico, South America, the United States, and beyond. Some believed human satanic cults were responsible for the carnage. Some believe Chupacabras came from outer space. But Chupacabra expert and writer Ben Radford has another theory.

In his book, *Tracking the Chupacabra: The Vampire Beast in Fact, Fiction, and Folklore*, Radford confirms that Tolentino saw the science fiction motion picture *Species* prior to seeing the mysterious creature detailed in her reports. Featured in the film is a green, bipedal monster called Sil—a monster with wraparound eyes and spinal spikes.

Did Tolentino's subconscious mind see a shadowy figure and draw from what she'd seen in the film? Or did she see a real, blood-sucking creature? Without more evidence, it's hard to know. But the Chupacabra is one of the most popular cryptids in the field.

Juvenile Chupacabra

Cryptkins Come to Life

When Cryptozoic Entertainment announced Cryptkins, a series of vinyl blind-box toys, collectors were thrilled. Baby cryptids, including Nessie, Chupacabra, Bigfoot and ten others sculpted by Sam Greenwell, were adorable.

"Think Littlest Pet Shop meets monsters," said Cryptozoic marketing coordinator Krystyl Chwa. Sold in cardboard crates with trading cards, they were an instant success.

Why Greenwell? "He's an insanely skilled sculptor," Chwa said. "We wanted the Cryptkins to be cute and creepy all at once." Greenwell met the challenge.

Where did this concept come from? "Our team grew up on legends, folklore, and mythology about mysterious creatures," Chwa said on her blog. "The name Cryptkins was inspired by our company name."

"The concept art took about three months of work to finalize," Chwa explained. "To go from concept to collectible on the shelf took about eleven months."

Not every mystery made the final list. "Lizardman, Roswell Aliens, Melon Head failed to make the cut," Chwa said. "But there are some I won't mention, because they will be appearing in the Series Two."

The creatures also have a digital side. "Through the Cryptkins Channel on Quidd," said CEO John Sepenuk, "people can explore these characters' colorful personalities." Digital stickers bring them to life.

Want more information? Follow the little monsters @Cryptkins on Instagram and Twitter.

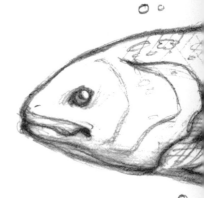

COELACANTH

(SEE-lah-canth)

FIRST REDISCOVERED:	1938
LOCATION:	INDIAN OCEAN, INDONESIA
CRYPTID TYPE:	AQUATIC; FISH-LIKE
REALITY RATING:	★ ★ ★ ★ ★

FACTOID: According to the Smithsonian Institution, there were once more than ninety species of coelacanth, a primitive, lobe-finned giant that once swam the waters of the prehistoric earth worldwide—in both salt and fresh waters. Today, only two species survive as living fossils.

EYEWITNESS ACCOUNT: The coelacanth was thought to be a victim of extinction sixty-five million years ago. It vanished, scientists thought, along with the dinosaurs, flying reptiles,

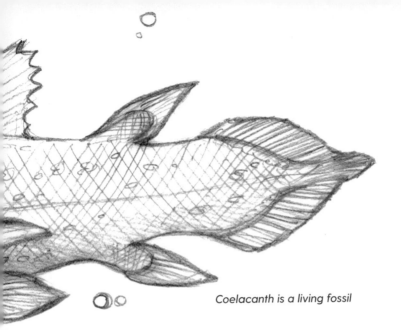

Coelacanth is a living fossil

and marine reptiles of ancient eras. In 1938, scientists realized they were wrong.

In December of that year, thirty-one-year-old museum curator Marjorie Courtenay-Latimer of East London, South Africa, was called to the local port by her friend, Captain Hendrick Goosen. The captain had returned from fishing the Indian Ocean on his trawler, the *Nerine*. If she found anything special from his catch, he explained, she could have it for her museum.

Marjorie was focused on beefing up the reptile exhibit but decided to travel to the docks to wish her friend a merry Christmas. As she turned to leave, she noticed a shimmering blue fin protruding from among the rest of Captain Hendrick Goosen's catch.

*Coelacanth pups take a
year to hatch*

It was, she wrote in her journal, "the most beautiful fish
I had ever seen, five feet long and a pale mauve blue with
iridescent silver markings." She discovered that the coelacanth
had escaped extinction.

Today, colonies of this living fossil survive near the
Comoros Islands in the Indian Ocean (between the east coast of
Africa and Madagascar), and in northern Sulawesi, Indonesia—
nearly six thousand miles east of the Comoros Islands.

Fully grown, a six-foot-long, two-hundred-pound coelacanth
lives in the "twilight zone" or the deepest part of its habitat, up
to 2,300 feet deep. It feeds on cephalopods—cuttlefish, squid,
and octopus—along with smaller fish found among undersea
volcanic slopes and caves.

Male and female coelacanths mate via internal fertilization of eggs. A year later, the pups emerge fully formed after feeding on yolk sacks. Only two females have been studied while carrying young; one carried six fourteen-inch pups, the other carried twenty-six.

Though the coelacanth is not a terribly intelligent creature—its brain fills only one-and-a-half percent of its cranial cavity, according to *National Geographic*, and the rest is filled with fat—it can live up to sixty years, if left undisturbed.

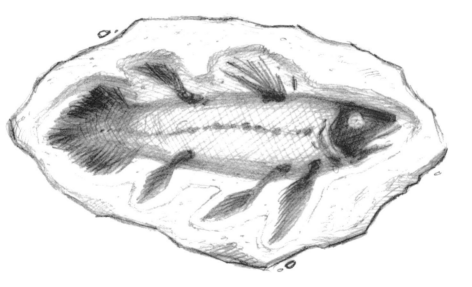

Prehistoric adult coelacanth fossil

Con Rit, a centipede larger than any known shark

CON RIT

(con RIT)

FIRST REPORTED:	1883
LOCATION:	GULF OF TONKIN, VIETNAM
CRYPTID TYPE:	AQUATIC; INSECT-LIKE
REALITY RATING:	★ ★ ★

FACTOID: *Con rit* is the Vietnamese word for centipede— a segmented arthropod of class Chilopoda. According to the *Guinness World Records* website, the largest centipede in the modern world is the ten-inch venomous *Scolopendra gigantea* of Central and South America. But the largest living centipede would be dwarfed by the Con Rit.

EYEWITNESS ACCOUNT: Ancient folklore in North Vietnam and Southern China called the Con Rit a holy water dragon with a segmented body. More recent accounts describe it as a fifty- to one-hundred-foot centipede gliding through the oceans of Southeast Asia.

According to cryptozoologist Loren Coleman's book, *Cryptozoology A to Z*, a Vietnamese man touched the lifeless

Con Rit may have been an oarfish (pictured here)

body of a Con Rit when it washed to shore in the Gulf of Tonkin in 1883. Many years later, Dr. A. Krempf, the director of the Oceanographic and Fisheries Service of Indochina in the 1920s, interviewed the eyewitness.

The dark-brown carcass was allegedly sixty feet long and three feet wide with two-foot armored segments protecting the entire length of its body. A pair of two-foot legs or filaments protruded from each segment. The belly was described as pale yellow or cream colored. When the body began to stink, a local fisherman towed it out to sea and abandoned it.

Juvenile Con Rit imagined

Bernard Heuvelmans, commonly known as the father of cryptozoology, wrote about the possibility of the Con Rit being an ancient armored whale that escaped earlier extinction. Zoologist and cryptozoology expert Dr. Karl Shuker suggests it could be a giant isopod—an aquatic centipede not yet scientifically identified. Others suggest it might have been a misidentified oarfish.

Physical evidence has not yet been discovered, so the Con Rit remains a true mystery.

DINGONEK

(DING-oh-nek)

FIRST REPORTED:	1907
LOCATION:	KENYA AND SOUTH AFRICA
CRYPTID TYPE:	AQUATIC; CAT-LIKE
REALITY RATING:	★ ★

FACTOID: Though most experts consider the Dingonek to be the stuff of legends, one unconfirmed report suggests a painting in a cave in South Africa matches the cryptid's description almost exactly.

EYEWITNESS ACCOUNT: Eyewitness accounts are difficult to verify when it comes to the "Jungle Walrus," also known as the Dingonek. One story is often repeated,

Could the "Jungle Walrus" be a big cat?

Adult Dingonek skull

with little reliable sourcing. So while we share it here, its credibility is uncertain.

Explorer John Alfred Jordan supposedly saw the cryptid in 1907 in Kenya. Jordan's guide spotted it first on the banks of the River Maggori. He led his employer to the river's edge to witness the fearsome beast. When Jordan saw the monster, he shot, but only grazed an ear. The angry Dingonek roared as the frightened men ran away.

Adventure author Edgar Beecher Bronson recounted Jordan's alleged encounter as a shared fireside chat in his 1910 book, *In Closed Territory.*

"Holy saints, but he was a sight," Bronson wrote, quoting Jordan. "Fourteen or fifteen feet long, head big as that of a lioness but shaped and marked like a leopard, two long white fangs sticking down straight out of his upper jaw, back as broad as a ship, scaled like an armadillo, but colored and marked like a leopard, and a broad fin tail, with slow lazy swishes of which he was easily holding himself level in the swift current, headed up stream."

Bronson died in 1917, so it's impossible to collect more details about Jordan's experience. As a result, this Dingonek story remains inconclusive.

Dingonek cub

Was the Dobhar-chú an otter?

DOBHAR-CHÚ

(dib-HAR-chew)

FIRST REPORTED:	**1684**
LOCATION:	**CREEVELEA, IRELAND**
CRYPTID TYPE:	**AQUATIC; OTTER-LIKE**
REALITY RATING:	★ ★ ★

FACTOID: Ireland's "hound of the deep," Dobhar-chú has a history more than three hundred and fifty years long. But some local immigrants believe the man-eating beast followed them from Ireland to the United States to wreak havoc in Lake Erie by a new name, the lake monster Bessie.

EYEWITNESS ACCOUNT: Irish journalist Rachel Rafferty told the story of Dobhar-chú on a website known as Ireland of the Welcomes. While her story is detailed, it's difficult to validate its credibility.

Rafferty suggests that Dobhar-chú means "water hound" and looks like a cross between an oversized otter and a dog, roughly seven feet long. It is rumored to live in and around the lakes of the British Isles and is sometimes considered the Irish cousin of Scotland's Loch Ness Monster.

Historic eyewitness accounts suggest Dobhar-chú has a taste for human flesh and the speed and agility to cut prey down with ease. They often live in pairs, and if one is wounded or killed, the other will avenge its partner by going after the human assassin.

Adult Dobhar-chú skull

Grace Connolly of Creevelea, Ireland, allegedly saw the beast on September 22, 1722. While washing her clothes in the lake, the monster sprang out of the water and killed the woman.

Her husband, Terence, drew his dagger to end the creature's life. As the Dobhar-chú died, it let out a scream to alert its mate, which came to avenge its partner. Terence jumped on his horse, but the Dobhar-chú continued the chase on dry land.

A blacksmith in a nearby town told Terence to stop running and use a sword to kill the giant beast. He took the advice and dispatched the second Dobhar-chú as he had the first.

Grace Connolly's gravestone still stands in the Conwall cemetery in the town of Drummans, Ireland. The Dobhar-chú that killed her is carved in the headstone's face. The Dobhar-chú bodies are allegedly buried nearby in the Sligo region of Ireland.

A more recent eyewitness account took place in 2003, when Irish artist Sean Corcoran and his wife crossed the Dobhar-chú's path in Omey Island, Connemara.

"We had come across the island by pure accident," Corcoran said. "But as soon as we found Omey, we were hooked. We spent an eventful few weeks puttering around the island by day and lounging by campfire at night. It was a very peaceful day until something strange happened."

As Corcoran and his wife slept, a strange noise erupted. "I strapped on my little head torch and we crept out in the pitch black. We heard a vicious snarl, a loud hiss, and a huge splash. I tried my best to keep my head steady to see what it was. It swam the width of the lake from west to east in what seemed like seconds. It moved quietly, but left a fairly big wake."

When the mystery creature got to the other side of the lake, it climbed onto a boulder and stared at the young couple. "It turned, stood up on its hind legs, and gave the most haunting screech. Its body was dark, about the size of a large Labrador—about five foot tall standing. Then it disappeared into the darkness."

When they shared the story with local residents, the Corcorans were told they'd seen a local legend—the mysterious Dobhar-chú.

Dobhar-chú pup

DOVER DEMON

(DOE-ver Demon)

FIRST REPORTED:	1972
LOCATION:	MASSACHUSETTS, UNITED STATES
CRYPTID TYPE:	TERRESTRIAL; HUMANOID-LIKE
REALITY RATING:	★ ★ ★ ★

FACTOID: When the Dover Demon was sighted in 1977, all three witnesses spotted it near water, and all three locations, when plotted on a map, were in a straight line.

EYEWITNESS ACCOUNT: According to the *Boston Globe*, Mark Sennott and his friends were students at Dover-Sherborn High School when they first spotted what may have been the Dover Demon in Massachusetts in 1972.

"We saw a small figure, deep in the woods, moving at the edge of the pond," he said. "We didn't know—it could have been an animal."

Five years later, William Bartlett and two other teens really put the Dover Demon on the map.

Dover Demon may have been an alien

Around 10:00 p.m. on April 21, 1977, seventeen-year-old Bartlett was driving when he saw a bizarre creature perched on a stone wall. At midnight, John Baxter, fifteen, got within fifteen feet of what experts believe was the same creature. Fifteen-year-old Abby Brabham spotted it the next night, driving home with her boyfriend.

All three described the same key features to police. It was about four feet tall, had an egg-shaped head, glowing red or orange eyes, and no mouth or nose. It wasn't an ordinary animal, they said—not a moose or a fox. They'd grown up around the region's animal life. This was no animal.

It looked more like a kid with a distended belly, Bartlett said, a kid with terrifying eyes. While filing his police report, he drew a sketch of what he'd seen and wrote a cryptic declaration on the page: "I, Bill Bartlett swear on a stack of Bibles that I saw this creature."

Few sightings have been documented since. As a middle-aged adult and a fine artist who exhibits his paintings

A glimpse inside the space suit

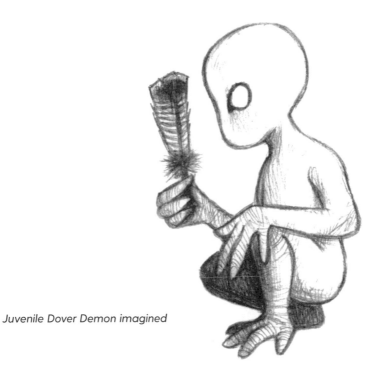

Juvenile Dover Demon imagined

regularly, being eyewitness to a monster hasn't been easy for Bartlett. People who have known him all his life think he saw something like the Easter Bunny, something unreal. But he stands by his story.

"In a lot of ways, it's kind of embarrassing to me," he said in the *Boston Globe*. "It was definitely weird. I didn't make it up. Sometimes, I wish I had."

Drop Bear imagined

DROP BEAR

(drop bayr)

FIRST REPORTED:	**2005**
LOCATION:	**PERTH, AUSTRALIA**
CRYPTID TYPE:	**TERRESTRIAL; KOALA-LIKE**
REALITY RATING:	★

FACTOID: Australians are eager to share information about this mysterious koala cousin. Like the koala, it is arboreal, or tree-dwelling. But they say it is a meat eater—it couldn't care less about the koala's eucalyptus leaves. It hates Vegemite, a popular Australian snack food. And the slogan, "Look up, stay alive," was created in the Drop Bear's honor.

EYEWITNESS ACCOUNT: According to legend—and the Australian Museum's website—the Drop Bear is a ferocious, large-dog-size koala cousin lurking in the continent's high places. Lying in wait, the sharp-toothed carnivore lingers until an unsuspecting meal gets close. Without warning, it drops from its perch to make the kill.

"The initial impact often stuns the prey, allowing it to be bitten on the neck and quickly subdued," the Australian Museum's website says.

Adult Drop Bear skull

Local experts are quick to warn hiking tourists of the Drop Bear danger. Foreign visitors quake at the thought of a giant killer koala ending their lives and their vacations with one swipe. But could such a beast really exist?

Apparently, the answer is no—at least not in this geologic era. Most experts down under agree the Drop Bear is a fiction created for the fun of scaring tourists. But there are times when the facts and fiction intersect.

When paleontologists found a stash of bones inside southwestern Australia's Tight Entrance Cave, it included an intriguing Ice Age marsupial named *Thylacoleo carnifex*— translation, "marsupial lion." To their delight, its articulated bones closely resemble the description of the fictional Drop Bear.

Thylacoleo wasn't really a lion. It was a marsupial, like kangaroos, wombats, koalas, and possums. The paws of *Thylacoleo* were equipped with powerful claws; it could have

easily climbed trees or steep rock faces to hunt or rest. Claw marks within the cave confirmed the power of its pounce.

So while the Drop Bear was never real, the *Thylacoleo* surely filled its niche two and a half million years ago.

Adult *Thylacoleo skull*

Rockstar's Bigfoot Easter Egg

Rockstar is famous for surprises known as "Easter eggs" into their video games code. But *Grand Theft Auto V* in 2013 featured one of the greatest Easter eggs of all time—the chance to hunt and play as a Sasquatch.

Unlocking the prize wasn't easy. According to a 2016 report on Kotaku.com, the clues were well hidden. But a team of code readers called the "Codewalkers" slowly pieced together the requirements.

According to one of the players on the quest, this was all very difficult, because Rockstar technicians are masters at hiding their code.

Rockstar was also cagey. One hint hidden in the code read, "He was wrong to start his hunt on Tuesday." But what did that mean? Gamers eventually discovered a golden peyote plant would only spawn on a Tuesday when it was foggy or snowy.

Three years after the game was released, the path was revealed. Seven different peyote plants had to be found and consumed to unlock the Sasquatch hunt option. If players spared the Sasquatch from a bloody death, they could actually play as the Sasquatch.

If they went the extra mile, and players could tackle *GTA V* as a furry character in a letter jacket that looked a lot like Michael J. Fox in the classic film *Teen Wolf*.

FOUKE MONSTER

(FOWk Monster)

FIRST REPORTED:	1908
LOCATION:	ARKANSAS, UNITED STATES
CRYPTID TYPE:	TERRESTRIAL; APE-LIKE
REALITY RATING:	★ ★ ★ ★

FACTOID: Searching for Fouke Monster trinkets? Visit the Monster Mart, a store and museum on Arkansas's Highway 71, just fifteen miles southeast of Texarkana.

EYEWITNESS ACCOUNT: Fouke, Arkansas, is a very small town—little more than eight hundred people call it home. But fame has visited Fouke, thanks to the legendary Fouke Monster, also known as the Boggy Creek Monster. The earliest known report was recorded in 1908, but an event in 1971 put the creature on the cryptozoological map.

Elizabeth Ford was sleeping on the family couch late on the night of May 2 when she heard a commotion. She woke to see the furry arm of what she thought was a bear breaking through the screen window.

Fouke Monster inspired a horror film

Her husband, Bobby, and his brother Don were outside and heard Elizabeth scream. They ran to her aid and saw the animal standing seven feet tall at the window.

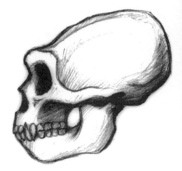

Adult Fouke Monster skull

"I felt a hairy arm come over my shoulder," Bobby said, "and the next thing I knew we were on the ground. The only thing I could think about was to get out of there." In a panic, he ran through the wood-and-glass front door, without opening it.

Even so, the men managed to empty their guns, firing several shots toward the foul-smelling creature to scare it away. They thought they'd hit the animal that rapidly escaped, but no trace of blood was found. The search did turn up three-toed footprints, scratch marks, and damage to the screen and siding on the house.

In the weeks that followed, several other people reported seeing an ape-like creature, so Little Rock, Arkansas, radio station KAAY offered more than $1,000 bounty for the first person to produce definitive evidence. The money went unclaimed.

Radio wasn't the only entertainment medium paying attention to the Fouke Monster. Filmmaker Charles B. Pierce saw money in the making and released *The Legend of Boggy Creek*, a horror movie loosely based on eyewitness reports, in 1972. The frightening low-budget film quickly grossed $20 million, and several sequels followed.

But not every witness sees the Fouke Monster as a danger. William Lundsford was seventeen when he saw the monster a few years later while fishing. "He began to stand up and he lifted this branch and he kept standing and kept standing and he kept standing. And I immediately just freeze," he told a reporter for Fox 16 News in 2015.

"I can't hardly breathe. There's tears that are streaming down my face and I've actually wet my pants," he said, recalling the story to the reporter, Susanne Brunner, as if it was happening. "I can see everything just as it happened, I can feel everything. It's been so many years ago, but it's so [affected] my life."

Lundsford became an amateur Bigfoot researcher as a

Fouke Monster juvenile

result of that life-changing event, and he's not alone. Brunner received a photo of what appears to be a Fouke Monster with a baby clinging to its side from another witness, a photo Lundsford says looks very much like the animal he saw.

Could the Fouke Monster be the local name for Bigfoot? And could the creature be real? The people of Fouke are willing to keep an open mind until indisputable evidence is nailed down.

A Giant Hare, as compared to an ordinary rabbit's silhouette

GIANT HARE

(JI-ant hare)

FIRST REPORTED:	**1976**
LOCATION:	**DORSET, ENGLAND**
CRYPTID TYPE:	**TERRESTRIAL; HARE-LIKE**
REALITY RATING:	★ ★ ★

FACTOID: The Giant Hare isn't the only bunny-like cryptid. The jackalope—a jackrabbit with antlers—is another, even if it's not real. Taxidermist Douglas Herrick invented the jackalope with his brother in Wyoming in the 1930s. But their inspiration may have been rooted in fact. Ordinary rabbits infected with the Shope papilloma virus grow tumors that look like horns and antlers on their heads and other body parts.

EYEWITNESS ACCOUNT: In 1976, British citizen Louise Hodgson was wandering the wilds of Dorset when she met a group of travelers and their dogs. They continued to explore together until Hodgson spotted something remarkable.

"We came to a blind valley and it was early September, so it was an unusual sight for that time of year," she said in a 2018 interview for the British newspaper *Daily Express*, "but there was a group of ten to thirteen hares with what we thought was a deer."

When they looked closer, Hodgson realized there was no deer, but rather a giant-size hare. "It was a wonderful experience," Hodgson said. "It shows there are still some secrets in nature."

British paranormal expert Marian Green says such mysteries aren't as unusual as we think. "In the countryside, many things happen. The king or queen hares are out there," she told Hodgson at a conference in February of 2018. What Hodgson saw was real, Green insisted.

"So are fairies, elemental spirits, and ghosts," she continued. "Some want to speak with us again, connect with us again, and we can be oblivious to what is going on around us."

Cryptozoologist Dr. Karl Shuker believes other people have also seen giant rabbits— two in Banbury, Oxfordshire, and one in Felton, Northumbria. But he doubts they were supernatural. More likely they were escaped domesticated breeds. The Flemish Giant rabbit can grow as long as three feet and weigh twenty-five pounds.

Adult Giant Hare skull

Giant Hare kit

There is a big difference between a three-foot rabbit and an adult deer, so Hodgson may be skeptical of Shuker's theory. But perhaps she's revealed more information in her book, *Secret Places of West Dorset*. A deer-sized rabbit could be an excellent magical companion.

GOATMAN

(goat-man)

FIRST REPORTED:	**1957**
LOCATION:	**MARYLAND, UNITED STATES**
CRYPTID TYPE:	**TERRESTRIAL; GOAT-LIKE**
REALITY RATING:	★ ★

FACTOID: The modern Goatman came back into focus in 1971, but the earliest stories are far more ancient. Called the Satyr in the Greco-Roman era, it was the keeper of the woodlands and known for flirting.

EYEWITNESS ACCOUNT: Though the stories began centuries ago, the search for the Goatman took on new life in October of 1971, when the Edwards family dog, Ginger, disappeared in the deep woods of Prince George's County in Maryland. Sixteen-year-old eyewitness April Edwards and her friends heard strange noises, then

Adult Goatman skull

Goatman as described by eyewitnesses

spotted a mysterious figure in the brush just hours before the dog vanished.

Teenage boys later found the body of the dog, its severed head missing. The Goatman was blamed for the violence, and the stories took on new life as teenagers mounted Goatman hunts on warm, summer nights.

Rumors of science gone horribly wrong surfaced. The Goatman, people said, was a product of experiments at the Beltsville Research Agricultural Center, a facility sponsored by the United States Department of Agriculture. Those theories were immediately shot down by the same facility.

Journalist Karen Hosler, who originally covered the story of the Goatman and the missing dog, dug deep into the archives of the University of Maryland Folklore Department and found that the Goatman wasn't the only woodland mystery in Prince George's County.

Does the Goatman prowl the woods near Washington, DC? Local police still answer calls about the odd monster. But without solid evidence, it's impossible to confirm more than this—the stories live on.

Goatman kid

Real-Life Weeki Wachee Mermaids

Yearning to be a mermaid? You're in luck. The Weeki Wachee Springs State Park in Florida might be hiring.

Since 1947, women have been performing as mermaids in the aquarium-like spring. The "mermaids" were women in swimsuits with air hoses, interacting with fish and props for tourists. According to the *New York Times Magazine*, they were paid in food, free swimwear, and glory—not money.

In 1959, the mermaids were finally compensated in currency, but some of it went toward rent to live in the mermaid dorms. A team of thirty-five mermaids played football, shared picnics, and generally dazzled the more-than-decent crowds.

Today, no mermaid would be caught dead without her elaborate mermaid tail. And the Weeki Wachee pros even host special mermaid camps for girls and women. But don't worry if you can't travel to Florida to witness their watery wonders. These modern mermaids also perform on YouTube.

Hellhound, the demon dog

HELLHOUND

(HELL-hownd)

FIRST REDISCOVERED:	1682
LOCATION:	KENTUCKY, UNITED STATES
CRYPTID TYPE:	TERRESTRIAL; DOG-LIKE
REALITY RATING:	★ ★ ★

FACTOID: Stories of hellhounds allegedly inspired author Sir Arthur Conan Doyle to write *The Hound of the Baskervilles*, his third Sherlock Holmes mystery novel.

EYEWITNESS ACCOUNT: Fluffy, from the famed Harry Potter book series, may be the best-known hellhound of the modern era. Video games, such as Activision's *Call of Duty* have also featured hellhound zombies. But there are those who believe hellhounds walk the real world as ferociously as they do in works of fiction.

First referenced in Greek mythology centuries ago, hellhounds are supernatural dogs of exceptional strength and size, often with matted black fur and red eyes. In legends, they are ushers of the afterlife and a symbol of impending death. Some stories say a single sighting means death is near.

Others say three sightings seal your fate.

Though they are known worldwide, British expert and researcher Nick Stone has collected almost five hundred stories from the United Kingdom and other European countries, and most describe an evil beast, sometimes called the Black Shuck.

Adult Hellhound skull

But some paint them as protectors. In one story,a hellhound defended a young girl against the abuse of a religious leader in the village of Littleport, England. The beast died defending the girl, leaving its ghost to wander the countryside.

Most people believe the hellhound is either a living feral canine or an imaginary foe. Both theories could be true, as seen in an episode of *Mountain Monsters*. A Kentucky man allegedly caught a large dog-like creature seven feet long on cell phone video. After seeing the video, the bearded cryptid hunters investigated the Pike County, Kentucky hellhound known for feeding on local cattle. Odds are good these cryptids are actually aggressive wild or feral dogs.

Hellhound pup

HIBAGON

(HIGH-beh-gone)

FIRST REPORTED:	1970
LOCATION:	HIROSHIMA, JAPAN
CRYPTID TYPE:	TERRESTRIAL; APE-LIKE
REALITY RATING:	★ ★ ★ ★

FACTOID: In December of 1970, an unusually long trackway was found in the snow of Mount Hiba in Japan. The bipedal footprints of the Hibagon were not as large as the North American Sasquatch, but they were clearly left by a barefoot creature with an ape-like opposable thumb on each foot. They looked more like gorilla footprints than prints left by human beings.

EYEWITNESS ACCOUNT: The earliest recorded Hibagon sighting came in early 1970, when a group of eyewitness elementary students were hiking Mount Hiba in search of wild mushrooms. As they picked their fill, they reported a bipedal, ape-like beast crashing through the brush to jump

Hibagon: Japan's Bigfoot

out at them. It pounded its chest like a gorilla and snapped tree branches as if they were twigs.

The children ran back to their teacher in fear. When they returned to investigate, the creature had vanished, but the broken branches were everywhere—breaks elementary school students would be too weak to have caused.

Dozens of other sightings spurred a study by students at Kobe University in 1972, with disappointing results. But sightings continued until they abruptly ended in the 1980s.

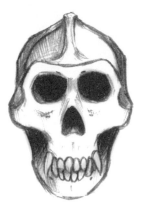

Adult Hibagon skull

The "Japanese bigfoot" was featured on American television in Jay Stephens' *The Secret Saturdays* episode titled "The Vengeance of the Hibagon," which ran on Cartoon Network in 2008.

Hibagon toddler

From Wolverine to Phineas

In December of 2017, *The Greatest Showman*, a musical story of P. T. Barnum starring *The Wolverine*'s Hugh Jackman, opened in theaters. It was a film seven years in the making.

Jackman really liked the script written by Jenny Bicks and Bill Condo, but investors weren't sure a musical would pay off.

"There's a huge part of the moviegoing audience who just won't go to a musical," Jackman told *Vogue* magazine, "so there's nervousness."

After more than a hundred meetings with studio executives, Twentieth Century Fox finally gave the film a green light. And the story of Phineas Taylor Barnum took flight. "It grew into a deeper idea, that what makes you different makes you special," Jackman said in *Vogue*.

"It's an incredible privilege to make a film about inclusivity and acceptance," director Michael Gracey continued. "It is Hugh's passion piece." And as Barnum himself said, "The noblest art is that of making others happy."

Hogzilla weighed 800 pounds or more

HOGZILLA

(HOG-zilla)

FIRST REPORTED:	2004
LOCATION:	GEORGIA, UNITED STATES
CRYPTID TYPE:	TERRESTRIAL; PIG-LIKE
REALITY RATING:	★ ★ ★ ★ ★ ★

FACTOID: Hogzilla was not the first giant hog to roam North America. The prehistoric pig *Daeodon shoshonensis* lived twenty-nine to nineteen million years ago, in the late Oligocene and early Miocene epochs. It was approximately seven feet tall at the shoulders and as much as twelve feet long. It weighed nearly half a ton and had a brain the size of an orange.

EYEWITNESS ACCOUNT: When explorer Christopher Columbus brought pigs to the Americas from Spain five hundred years ago, he couldn't have imagined they'd one day evolve to be predatory hybrids running wild in the rural South.

But hunting guide and eyewitness Chris Griffin can testify to their modern-day enormity. He shot the first documented pig/wild boar hybrid, dubbed Hogzilla, at his boss Ken Holyoak's fish farm and hunting reserve in Alapaha, Georgia, the summer of 2004.

Adult Hogzilla skull

"The plantation owner said he'd seen him several times," Griffin said on a radio interview, so he set out to bag it himself. Once Griffin shot it, measured it, and posed for a photo, he buried it, at Holyoak's instruction. "The hog was old and meat was no good," he said, and the head was too big and too expensive to mount. Burial seemed like the obvious solution.

Almost as soon as it was buried, people claimed the picture was a hoax. No wild hog had ever come in at twelve feet long and one thousand pounds in weight, they said. It must have been a domestic pig shot as a publicity stunt for the reserve. Nine months later, *National Geographic* and Dr. John J. Mayer stepped in to solve the mystery, exhuming the giant beast.

It came in a little smaller than Griffin's original measurements—seven and a half feet long and eight hundred pounds. But DNA tests proved it was a true pig/wild boar hybrid, not a pet.

How could they be sure? Tusks in domestic pigs are regularly filed down as a safety precaution. Hogzilla's tusks were twenty-eight inches and nineteen inches long, proving it was dangerous and anything but tame.

Other monstrous hybrids have been trophied since Hogzilla burst on the scene, including Son of Hogzilla, another Georgia beast shot by hunter Bill Coursey and his son Russell in Fayette County. It tipped the scale at 1,100 pounds, making it the largest wild hog ever discovered, according to Dr. Mayer. So the next time you hear something big rustling through the woods, just remember . . . it could be a giant of prehistoric proportions, like the *Daeodon shoshonensis*.

Baby Hogzilla

ILIAMNA LAKE MONSTER

(ill-ee-AHM-nah Lake Monster)

FIRST REPORTED:	1942
LOCATION:	ALASKA, UNITED STATES
CRYPTID TYPE:	AQUATIC; FISH-LIKE
REALITY RATING:	★ ★ ★ ★

FACTOID: Oil tycoon Tom Slick, who financed Yeti expeditions, offered a $1,000 bounty to any person who could prove Alaska's Iliamna Lake Monster was real. The search was unsuccessful.

EYEWITNESS ACCOUNT: According to a report in the *Juneau Empire* newspaper, Iliamna Lake, the largest body of fresh water in Alaska, is nearly eighty miles long and twenty-two miles wide. In most places, it is 660 feet deep, but in Pile Bay, the string used to measure the depth ran out at 985 feet, so it could have fallen far deeper—deep enough for a giant predator.

Iliamna Lake Monster, a Tlingit legend

For centuries, indigenous Alaskans have claimed to see the Iliamna Lake Monster swimming in its frosty waters. The Tlingit tribe told stories of an aquatic monster with the head and tail of a wolf and the body of an orca whale. A more recent telling came in 1942 from pilots Bill Hammersley and Babe Aylesworth.

While Hammersley flew a Stinson ferry plane above the lake, the two men spotted what appeared to be a group of very large fish at the surface of the water. They flew lower to get a closer look and realized the fish were larger than the sea plane's pontoons, with broad flat heads and dull gray bodies. Where most fish tails wave from side to side, these fish tails waved up and down, like a dolphin's.

*Iliamna Lake Monster may have been
a sturgeon (pictured here)*

Sports Afield magazine published an article called,
"Alaska's Monster Mystery Fish," with more than thirty
years' worth of eyewitness reports, in their January 1959
issue. The reports included Hammersley's follow-up attempt
to catch one of the fish using the flank of an adult moose as
bait. Whatever they hooked eventually snapped the sixteen-
inch stainless steel aircraft cable they used as fishing line and
got away with the meat.

The Animal Planet television network biologist and
fisherman Jeremy Wade sought the fish in an episode of *River
Monsters* called "Alaskan Horror." Almost immediately, he
eliminated pike or salmon as possible candidates. But he
decided it could be an enormous white sturgeon, which can
grow as big as twenty feet long.

Scientist Bruce Wright with the Aleutian Pribilof Islands Association has another theory. He believes the monster is a sleeper shark.

"Sleeper sharks surprise me all the time," he said in an interview. "They eat everything and anything. I've found chunks of gray whale, harbor seal, and even chrome chum salmon in their stomachs. They target the midsection to eviscerate their prey. Sure, they're cold blooded and slow moving, but they have their moments."

People have also seen the monster cruising the Kvichak River, which flows from Iliamna Lake on one end and into the Bering Sea's Bristol Bay on the other. So a sleeper shark could move from the ocean to the lake with ease.

Both theories are good, but neither is conclusive. So time and more evidence will be necessary to identify the monster for sure.

Another theory is the Iliamna Lake Monster may have been a sleeper shark (pictured here)

*Isothrix barbarabrownae was seen
only once, but is considered real*

ISOTHRIX BARBARABROWNAE

(EYE-soe-thrix bar-ba-ra-BROWN-ee)

FIRST REPORTED:	1999
LOCATION:	ANDES MOUNTAINS, PERU
CRYPTID TYPE:	TERRESTRIAL; SQUIRREL-LIKE
REALITY RATING:	★ ★ ★ ★ ★ ★

FACTOID: According to the International Institute for Species Exploration at Arizona State University, 18,500 new-to-science animal species were confirmed in 2007, but only 219 of those were mammals. Of these, eighty percent were long-extinct species known only from fossil remains. Finding new living mammals—like *Isothrix barbarabrownae*—is relatively rare.

EYEWITNESS ACCOUNT: In 1999, Field Museum scientist Bruce Patterson and his research team headed from Chicago to Manu National Park and Biosphere Reserve—6,200 feet high in the Andes Mountains of Southern Peru. They hoped to find new animal species during the ten-week field season. And they were successful.

High in the trees of the cloud forest, they found something remarkable: a brand new nocturnal rodent that had hidden in the trees undetected for centuries, if not millennia.

The size of a very large squirrel, the arboreal—or tree-dwelling—animal was part of the spiny rat family. It had dense brown fur with a black crest at the nape of the neck and shoulders. Unlike its nearest relative, the bush-tailed tree rat of South America's lowlands, this rodent had a long, thin tail covered in black fur with a white furry tip. In 2007, the new discovery was named *Isothrix barbarabrownae*.

"The new species is not only a handsome novelty," Patterson said in a Field Museum publication. "The newly discovered species casts a striking new light on the evolution of [. . .] arboreal rodents."

Patterson and his team returned for a second ten-week study in 2000 and a third in 2001. But they were unable to find a second specimen of the new species. As a result, how the creature actually lives is uncertain. Experts believe it eats seeds, berries, and insects, but likely never sets foot on the rain forest floor.

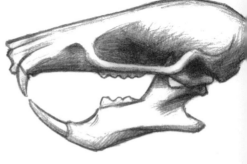

Adult Isothrix *skull*

Baby Isothrix

In time, the Field Museum may launch another search. Until then, *Isothrix barbarabrownae* will remain a real but rare mystery. How many of cryptozoology's mystery animals might turn out to be as real as *Isothrix barbarabrownae*—an animal seen only once with no physical evidence left behind? Only time will tell.

KASAI REX

(kah-SIGH recks)

FIRST REPORTED:	1932
LOCATION:	KASAI VALLEY, DEMOCRATIC REPUBLIC OF THE CONGO
CRYPTID TYPE:	TERRESTRIAL; LIZARD-LIKE
REALITY RATING:	★ ★

FACTOID: In 1932, a Zimbabwean newspaper, called the *Rhodesia Herald* at the time, ran a black-and-white photo of the *Kasai rex* that plantation owner John Johanson claimed to see in the Kasai Valley. But photo analysts believe it was a photo of a lizard superimposed onto an image of a dead rhinoceros.

EYEWITNESS ACCOUNT: Though unreliable, the story allegedly unfolded in 1932, in a region of Africa now known as the Democratic Republic of the Congo, when Swedish plantation owner John Johanson and his guide set out to hunt one of the territory's wild beasts on a quiet afternoon.

Adult Kasai rex

Adult Kasai rex *skull*

Johanson spotted a rhino grazing and aimed his rifle to bag the unsuspecting creature. But before he could squeeze the trigger, another animal burst out of the rain forest brush and attacked the rhino. Johanson was so upset by the sight, he fainted as his guide ran to safety.

When Johanson came to, he reportedly saw what looked like a *Tyrannosaurus* feeding on the dead rhino. It was red with black stripes, the legend suggests, with a long tail and dagger-like teeth. Approximately forty-three feet long, its footprints measured five feet long and more than two feet wide.

A second sighting was allegedly reported in a magazine that same year. And years later, two photos circulated as "proof" of the *Tyrannosaurus*'s authenticity. One proved to be a magazine lizard. The other was an image from the famous 1969 Ray Harryhausen stop-motion movie masterpiece, *Valley of the Gwangi*, pasted to a picture of a rhino.

Sources for the *Kasai rex* stories are not considered credible evidence. So while proof of its being a hoax is unavailable, that seems the most likely explanation.

Kasai rex *hatchling*

Kongamato may have been a pterosaur

KONGAMATO

(KONG-ah-mat-oh)

FIRST REPORTED:	1923
LOCATION:	BANGWEULU WETLANDS, ZAMBIA
CRYPTID TYPE:	AERIAL/TERRESTRIAL; BAT-LIKE
REALITY RATING:	★ ★

FACTOID: Kongamato means "breaker of boats."

EYEWITNESS ACCOUNT: Pterosaurs—flying reptiles that shared the earth with dinosaurs in prehistoric ages—went extinct sixty-six million years ago. But some people living in modern-day Zambia, Angola, and the Republic of the Congo on the African continent believe at least one species lives on: a flying carnivore known as Kongamato.

Cryptozoology books and websites suggest a number of people had brushes with a black or red pterosaur with a four- to seven-foot wingspan. But confirmation with more reliable sources is evasive.

Author Frank Melland's 1923 book, *In Witchbound Africa,* describes Kongamato as a dangerous menace that soared over rivers, attacking small boats that threatened its territory.

Three other eyewitnesses described similar encounters in the 1930s, in 1956, and in 1957—the last claiming a gaping wound in his chest came from the pterosaur's claws in the Bangweulu swamps. The wounded man allegedly drew a picture of a Kongamato when asked what creature inflicted the bloody gashes, but the drawing was lost.

Some say the encounters were with misidentified birds or giant bats. Others insist what they saw truly was a surviving ancient species.

Could a giant flying reptile dominate the skies of modern-day Africa? It's hard to say. But paleontologists announced the discovery of a giant fossilized African pterosaur in May of 2010 in the *Telegraph*, a British newspaper. Named *Alanqa saharica*—phoenix of the Sahara—it ruled the African skies ninety-five million years ago with a wingspan of nearly twenty feet. Did it escape extinction? It will require a great deal more evidence to answer that question. So the mystery endures.

Adult Kongamato skull

Kongamato chick

KRAKEN

(CRA-kin)

FIRST REPORTED:	**1180**
LOCATION:	**TRØNDELAG, NORWAY**
CRYPTID TYPE:	**AQUATIC; SQUID-LIKE**
REALITY RATING:	★ ★ ★ ★

FACTOID: One report on the Kraken suggests it had a strange lure for gathering food—poop! The muddy "evacuation" was supposedly delicious to schools of fish. As they gathered to feast, they became the feast. The Kraken tentacles ensnared them and drove them into the monster's beak.

EYEWITNESS ACCOUNT: For centuries, sailors have told the tale of the Kraken, a tentacled sea monster so large it could be mistaken for an uncharted island. The story originated with Norway's King Sverre in 1180 and quickly spread to Iceland, Greenland, and far beyond.

When unsuspecting ships drew too close, they would be wrapped in the Kraken's powerful arms and pulled to

Kraken, a giant squid that terrorizes

their deaths, devoured by the beast, boat and all. Should a crew member escape the sinking ship, the whirlpool created by the boat's downward spiral would draw him to his watery fate.

Adult Kraken beak

If the ship was able to evade capture, the Kraken would swim in circles around the boat, creating such a powerful wake the craft would be reduced to splinters. The Kraken would then feed on the sailors fleeing the debris.

When scientist Carl Linnaeus first cataloged known animal species in his book *Systema Naturae*, in 1735, the Kraken stories were so popular that he included the creature as a mighty cephalopod. But many considered it more fiction than fact.

The monster took on new scientific prowess when Danish naturalist Japetus Steenstrup came upon a real giant cephalopod stranded on a Danish beach in 1853. Steenstrup couldn't carry the entire body back to his office, so he took extensive notes and harvested the animal's beak as proof.

Based on that discovery, Steenstrup documented a new species—*Architeuthis dux*, the giant squid sometimes known as the Kraken. The stories now had science in their corner. But was this specimen the same as the Kraken described in folklore? It's hard to say.

The giant squid has no real muscle power in its tentacles, so it's unlikely it could do harm to a ship or even a rowboat. The biggest known example is huge—almost sixty feet long—but far from the size of even the smallest known islands.

Should the Kraken image be downsized? Perhaps, but according to the US National Oceanic and Atmospheric Administration (NOAA), less than twenty percent of the ocean has been explored. With so much yet to be discovered, even the most devout scientist must admit, something bigger could be lurking—something that could make *Architeuthis dux* look pint-sized.

To be continued . . .

Kraken juvenile

A seven-foot humanoid lizard

LIZARD MAN OF SCAPE ORE SWAMP

(lizard man of SKEIP or swamp)

FIRST REPORTED:	1988
LOCATION:	SOUTH CAROLINA, UNITED STATES
CRYPTID TYPE:	TERRESTRIAL; LIZARD-LIKE
REALITY RATING:	★ ★

FACTOID: According to Lyle Blackburn's 2013 book, *Lizard Man: The True Story of the Bishopville Monster*, several Lizard Man witnesses, including Christopher Davis, have died of unnatural causes. Could there be a Lizard Man curse?

EYEWITNESS ACCOUNT: On June 29, 1988, seventeen-year-old Christopher Davis of Lee County, South Carolina, was driving home from his shift at McDonald's. A flat tire forced him to pull to the side of the road, where he had an encounter with what would soon be known as the Lizard Man of Scape Ore Swamp.

According to Davis, as he changed the tire a seven-foot humanoid lizard with red eyes and three fingers appeared from the woods and did serious damage to his 1976 Toyota Celica. "I ran into the car and as I locked it, the thing grabbed the door handle," he told the *Houston*

Adult Lizard Man skull

Chronicle. "It was strong and angry [. . .] and then he jumped on the roof of my car."

Davis started the car and gunned the engine as the monster's clawed fingers gripped the front windshield. "I sped up and swerved to shake the creature off."

Kenneth Orr, an airman stationed at Shaw Air Force Base, later claimed he had shot and wounded the Lizard Man, presenting scales and blood as evidence to the local police. Within two days he recanted his story, saying he simply wanted to keep the legend alive.

The stories essentially evaporated until the Syfy channel filmed an episode of *Fact or Faked: Paranormal Files* in the forest near Bishopville, South Carolina. Former FBI agent Ben Hansen revealed to a breathless audience a mysterious video of the creature walking through the woods.

It was a fake. "We filmed what I call an ethical hoax," Hansen told the *Huffington Post*, "as a kind of social experiment. The whole idea was to see how much buzz we could generate."

Lizard Man hatchling

The production company hired a special effects expert to create a costume Hansen wore as he traipsed through the forest, careful not to provoke any local hunters.

The episode was all but duplicated in August of 2015 when a woman known only as Sarah from Sumter spotted the reptilian biped as she left church in Bishopville—and captured it on her cell phone camera.

"My hand to God," she said in a statement drafted for ABC News 4 WCIV in Mount Pleasant, South Carolina, "I am not making this up. So excited!" Her photo, which resembled a 1960s *Star Trek* costume, filled others with doubt, including Hansen, who believes the report is "dubious at best," according to the *Huffington Post*.

LOCH NESS MONSTER

(LOCK ness monster)

FIRST REPORTED:	565 CE
LOCATION:	LOCH NESS, SCOTLAND
CRYPTID TYPE:	AQUATIC; LAKE MONSTER-LIKE
REALITY RATING:	★ ★ ★

FACTOID: Nine-year-old Sam Knight may have captured a picture of the Loch Ness Monster's fin in November of 2017. While in Scotland on holiday, he toured the lake with a rope, a DNA kit, and a camera. He didn't get close enough to use the rest of his equipment, but his photograph made him world famous—at least for a few days. Sam was one of eight Loch Ness Monster eyewitnesses in 2017 alone.

EYEWITNESS ACCOUNT: Members of the Pictish tribe were among the first to inhabit the land known as Scotland. They may also have been the first to document the Loch Ness Monster. Dozens of stone reliefs carved in the sixth century are scattered across the countryside near the lake.

Nessie, Scotland's favorite monster

Every animal carved is readily recognizable—all but one, known as the Pictish Beast. Some believe the Pictish Beast is the Loch Ness Monster.

As the Picts began to convert to Christianity, another sighting marked the monster's history. After it allegedly caught and consumed a local farmer in 565 CE, Saint Columba commanded it to never feed on humanity again. Legend suggests it obeyed his command.

Adult Nessie skull

Rumors spread for centuries, but the next reliable witness was Dr. R. K. Wilson. As the road on the north shore of the lake was being constructed in 1933, drilling and explosives were required to carve out the rock. Perhaps the Loch Ness Monster was disturbed by the commotion enough to resurface. Dr. Wilson captured one of the most famous Nessie photographs ever recorded when it did.

The Loch Ness Investigation Bureau spent ten years conducting an observational survey in the 1960s and 1970s. Collecting well-documented evidence was the only way to confirm that something remarkable lived in the waters. An average of twenty sightings a year inspired a new way to search—a submarine. One photograph of what appears to be an aquatic flipper was produced, but no conclusive evidence has been found.

Debate is fierce on what Nessie might actually be. Some suggested it was a prehistoric plesiosaur, a throwback to the days of the dinosaur. But the lake was carved by a receding Ice Age glacier. It is extremely deep and filled with cold water.

Reptiles like the plesiosaur require warmth to digest their food. Ancient marine reptiles lived in warm, tropical waters. If a colony now filled the lake, they'd require external heat to survive—sunlight. They'd be seen often, basking in the sun to engage their metabolism. So strike the plesiosaur.

Nessie baby

Prehistoric whales and sea lions did very well in frigid waters. So do contemporary species, but very few are caught sunning on the shores of Loch Ness. Scratch whales and sea lions.

What could be lurking in the depths of the Loch Ness? Could it be a giant eel or a sturgeon of exceptional size? It's uncertain, but one thing is clear. We may need a few more centuries of observation to find out.

Loveland Frog with sparkling wand

LOVELAND FROG

(LOVE-land frog)

FIRST REPORTED:	1955
LOCATION:	LOVELAND, OHIO
CRYPTID TYPE:	AQUATIC/ TERRESTRIAL; FROG-LIKE
REALITY RATING:	★ ★

FACTOID: Ohio actor Joshua Steele grew up hearing stories of the Loveland Frog, a bizarre biped creature standing three feet high. "I was really attracted to the localism of this thing," Steele said of the cryptid in *USA Today*'s Cincinnati.com, so he and fellow actor Mike Hall created a stage musical about the creature. Audiences flocked to see it during the Cincinnati Fringe Festival in May and June of 2014.

EYEWITNESS ACCOUNT: It can't be confirmed, but the first sighting of the Loveland Frog was said to be in 1955 along the Little Miami River in Ohio. A weary anonymous businessman saw three bipedal frogs standing on the side of the road after midnight, waving a sparkling wand over their heads. The man claimed they had leathered bumpy skin and smelled like almonds.

Without the businessman's name, it's difficult to confirm the credibility of that story, but in 1972 another sighting brought the Loveland Frog back into focus.

Police Officer Ray Shockey was driving toward Loveland, Ohio, at 1:00 a.m. on March 3, 1972, when he saw a strange creature standing three to four feet tall, weighing roughly sixty pounds. It had leathery skin and a face like a frog or a lizard.

Officer Mark Mathews went back to look for evidence and found scrape marks leading down the hill toward the river, but there was no sign of the mysterious frogman. That is, until March 17, 1972, when Officer Mathews spotted the frogman and fired his revolver.

For years, Mathews swore he missed. But when a new witness turned up in August of 2016, he stepped forward with a new statement.

Adult Loveland Frog skull

Pokémon Go player Sam Jacobs claimed he spotted the Loveland Frog between Loveland Madeira Road and Lake Isabella. "The thing stood up and walked on its hind legs," he told WCPO News in Cincinnati. "I realize this sounds crazy, but I swear on my grandmother's grave this is the truth. The frog stood about four feet tall."

Loveland Frog tadpole

Impossible, Officer Mathews said, "I shot it." If Mathews shot the only living Loveland Frog, he could be right. He recovered the creature's lifeless body in 1972 and put it in his trunk. It was identified as a sickly iguana about three feet long. Officer Shockey agreed it was the creature he saw a few days earlier.

Sam Jacobs believes Officer Mathews shot what he saw that night in the early 1970s. But he insists what he saw in 2016 was no iguana. Did Jacobs see the real Loveland Frog? He isn't sure.

"Either way," he says, "I've never seen anything like it."

MAROZI

(mar-oh-ZEE)

FIRST REPORTED:	1903
LOCATION:	NAIROBI, KENYA
CRYPTID TYPE:	TERRESTRIAL; CAT-LIKE
REALITY RATING:	★ ★ ★ ★ ★

FACTOID: Though it has never happened in the wild, lions and leopards have been crossbred in captivity to create leopons. Their coats are very similar to the Marozi pelts allegedly collected in Kenya in 1931.

EYEWITNESS ACCOUNT: According to the March 20, 1963 edition of *Boys' Life* magazine, the tale of the Marozi was first shared with the modern world in 1903 when the people native to Kenya told British officer Richard Meinertzhagen about the big cat.

"The Marozis are not lions," the Kenyans said in the article. "There is the leopard, and there is the cheetah. There is the lion, and there is the Marozi."

Adult Marozi

Explorers in the decades that followed told stories of near brushes with the elusive spotted lions. But Aberdare Mountains farmer Michael Trent accidentally trapped one in an animal snare in 1931. When its mate arrived to defend her, Trent was forced to kill them both.

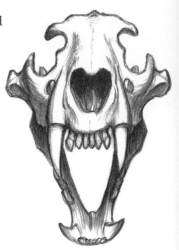

Adult Marozi skull

He skinned the big cats and saved the pelts, but he didn't think much about them until a game warden saw them and marveled at their unusual spots. The warden took the pelts to the Nairobi Game Department, where no one could identify the unusual species. They haven't been seen since.

Today, cryptozoologists have several theories on what the Marozi actually was. Some say it was a big cat hybrid, a lion and a leopard crossbreed. Such mating is extremely rare and only occurs when more traditional coupling is impossible due to vanishing populations.

Lions and leopards have been bred in captivity, but according to *National Geographic*, such genetic manipulation can be unethical and ill-advised.

Others maintain the Marozi was a shy, unique species of its own. In 1955, the Belgian scientist, Dr. Bernard Heuvelmans, proposed naming the spotted lion *Leo maculatus.*

Trent's missing pelts may be a part of the National History Museum collections in London. But unless DNA tests are done, the animal's true identity will remain a legendary African mystery.

Marozi cub

MEGALODON

(MEG-ah-LOW-don)

FIRST REDISCOVERED:	2013
LOCATION:	CALIFORNIA, UNITED STATES
CRYPTID TYPE:	AQUATIC; SHARK-LIKE
REALITY RATING:	★ ★ ★ ★

FACTOID: Sharktooth Hill in Bakersfield, California, is the richest bone bed for Miocene marine life fossils, including the prehistoric Megalodon shark, known only by its teeth. In fact, Megalodon literally means "big tooth."

EYEWITNESS ACCOUNT: That the sixty-foot-long Megalodon did exist is not in question. The behemoth shark did swim Earth's ancient oceans until 2.6 million years ago, when it

Did the prehistoric Megalodon survive?

went extinct. But with less than twenty percent of the ocean fully explored, speculation continues. Could the prehistoric giant still be alive?

Discovery Channel asked that question in a "documentary" in 2013. Producer Michael Sorensen described it this way for CNN: "We wanted to explore the possibilities of Megalodon. It's one of the most debated shark discussions of all time. It's [the] ultimate *Shark Week* fantasy."

Almost five million viewers tuned in to join Sorensen in that exploration, making it one of the highest-rated *Shark Week* programs in history. The network did offer

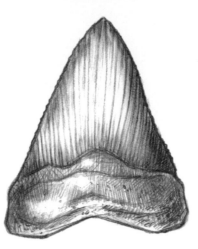

Adult Megalodon teeth could be up to seven inches long

disclaimers—"Certain events and characters in this film have been dramatized." But Sorensen suggested the stories had circulated for years. "Who really knows?" he said.

We do, answered an army of frustrated paleontologists and shark experts, who reaffirmed that Megalodon was long extinct. Even *Star Trek: The Next Generation* actor Wil Wheaton cried foul.

"Discovery had a chance to get its audience thinking about what the oceans were like when Megalodon roamed," Wheaton wrote. "But Discovery Channel did not do that [. . .] the network deliberately lied to its audience and presented fiction as fact."

Jonathan Downes, director of the Centre for Fortean Zoology, doubts Megalodon survived extinction. But he sees the debate as a distraction. There are new mysteries lurking in the sea, he says, including one shaped like a colossal tadpole.

"There's a lot of evidence to suggest that in the seas around Fiji there [is] a new species of these enormous sharks, bigger than whale sharks," he said in the *Daily Star* British newspaper. Considering the whale shark is thirty-two feet long and weighs in at more than forty thousand pounds, he's talking a really big beast. "It's either a different color of one we haven't discovered yet," he said, "or it is actually a completely new species of giant shark."

With vast expanses of ocean unknown to humankind, countless marine mysteries are bound to be revealed in years to come, assuming we keep our oceans healthy enough for them to escape the apparent fate of Megalodon. Monsters yet lurk, even if we aren't sure what kind.

Megalodon pup

Mermaids have enchanted people for centuries

MERMAID

(MER-maid)

FIRST RECORDED:	2000 BCE
LOCATION:	UNKNOWN
CRYPTID TYPE:	AQUATIC; HUMANOID-LIKE
REALITY RATING:	★ ★

FACTOID: According to C. J. S. Thompson, author of *The Mystery and Lore of Monsters*, the Babylonian fish-god Oannes is one of the earliest mermen in recorded history. "[It] is usually depicted as having a beaded head with a crown and a body like a man, but from the waist downwards he has the shape of a fish."

EYEWITNESS ACCOUNT: Mermaid stories are not new. Thessalonike, the half-sister of Alexander the Great, was so sad when he died in 323 BCE that she threw herself in the sea. Legend said she was transformed into a mermaid. The Greeks celebrated the son of Poseidon, Triton—a merman with a trident, a conch horn, and shoulders adorned with seashells. The Hindus had Suvannamaccha, the "golden fish" mermaid princess who fell in love with a human. And the

Blue Men of the Minch challenged sailors to rhyming contests off the ancient coast of Scotland. When the humans failed, the Blue Men sent them to their watery graves.

The stories endure, but could mermaids be real? Captain John Smith allegedly thought so. Author Edward Snow describes the encounter in his book, *Incredible Mysteries and Legends of the Sea.*

While at sea, Snow writes, Smith saw a mermaid, "swimming about with all possible grace." Endowed with large eyes, a petite nose, oversized ears, and "long green hair [that] imparted to her an original character that was by no means unattractive," the mermaid enchanted the captain, who felt "the first effects of love." Imagine his surprise when his love revealed her fishy secret.

Today, most experts have concluded mermaids were either works of fiction or cases of misidentification—like sea cows seen through a watery haze. But that didn't stop Animal Planet from launching its aquatic humanoids on May 27, 2012.

Manatees are often mistaken for mermaids

Mermaids: The Body Found introduced a theory of apes that had evolved into aquatic life-forms, represented in computer-animated sequences. Also featured was Dr. Paul Robertson, introduced as a former National Oceanic and Atmospheric Administration (NOAA) scientist. Robertson said he had evidence to prove mermaids were real, but that the evidence had been confiscated by the United States government.

When the show previously aired in 2011 in Australia, *Sydney Morning Herald* journalist Brad Newsome called it out. "It's not that there's anything wrong with a bit of speculative evolution," he wrote, "as long as you make it clear [. . .] that you're making stuff up."

NOAA released a statement saying, "no evidence of aquatic humanoids had ever been found," and confirmed that Dr. Paul Robertson was a character portrayed by an actor with no connection to the agency. The production was a hoax, as was its sequel, *Mermaids: The New Evidence.*

Many mysteries do lurk in the sea, animals of amazement we haven't yet discovered. But the odds are good that mermaids will not be among them.

MOMO

(MOE-moe)

FIRST REPORTED:	1971
LOCATION:	MISSOURI, UNITED STATES
CRYPTID TYPE:	TERRESTRIAL; HUMANOID-LIKE
REALITY RATING:	★ ★ ★ ★

FACTOID: Momo was so popular in the 1970s, entertainer Bill Whyte created the creature's musical anthem. "Some said it was a monster, some said it was a bear, but most of us could tell by that horrible smell that Momo had just been there."

EYEWITNESS ACCOUNT: Some accounts suggest Momo—the Missouri Monster—had an extra-wide pumpkin-shaped face, golden eyes, and the dark fur-covered body of a Sasquatch. But what sets this seven-foot-tall biped apart is its reportedly violent behavior.

Dozens of stories have been collected from the Mississippi River town of Louisiana, Missouri. One even had the creature lifting the back end of a compact car.

Momo, the shaggy Bigfoot

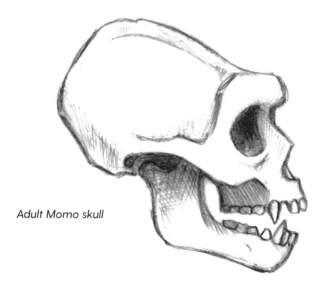

Adult Momo skull

But the most detailed and best-documented story was about the Harrison family encounter.

Doris Harrison Bliss was babysitting her two younger brothers one summer day when the boys ran into the house crying. They told her they'd seen a monster carrying a bloody dog in the yard. Though she didn't believe the boys, Doris went outside to investigate. She saw nothing.

When she came back inside, the boys built a makeshift blockade to protect themselves, while Doris got back to her chores. As she cleaned the bathroom sink, she saw Momo—a tall, hairy animal covered in brush—through the bathroom window. She did not see the bloody dog, but she was terrified by what she did see.

Doris called her father at work. He reassured her that it was probably their imaginations running away with them.

But a few days later, he and a small group of family friends heard a mysterious roar from the woods that made them believers.

In a 2012 interview, Doris denied it might have been a bear, bobcat, cougar, or mountain lion roar—it was much, much scarier.

After she married, only a short time later, Doris left her childhood home and never returned. She claims there was always some terrible noise and smell lurking around.

Neighbors made fun of the Harrison family after they reported the sighting to the local authorities. But Doris stands by her story. She doesn't care if they believe her.

Momo junior

Mothman has a museum of its own

MOTHMAN

(MOTH-man)

FIRST REPORTED:	**1966**
LOCATION:	**WEST VIRGINIA, UNITED STATES**
CRYPTID TYPE:	**AERIAL; HUMANOID-LIKE**
REALITY RATING:	★ ★ ★ ★

FACTOID: The Mothman Museum is the cryptozoological heart of Point Pleasant, West Virginia, just a mile off Interstate 35. Opened in 2005 by father-and-daughter team Jeff Wamsley and Ashley Watts, it features historic Mothman artifacts and interactive exhibits. Its entrance is just past the life-size metal Mothman sculpture outside.

EYEWITNESS ACCOUNT: On November 12, 1966, something strange descended on Point Pleasant, West Virginia. Five men digging a grave near Clendenin saw what they called a man-like creature take flight from a nearby tree—it was the first sighting of the legendary Mothman.

Three days later, Steve Mallette, Roger Scarberry, and their wives got a closer look. Sometime after 11:30 p.m., they saw a bipedal creature roughly seven feet tall, with wings. Both described a wingspan of ten feet and piercing eyes that glowed red in a beam of direct light, like a headlight.

Adult Mothman skull

"It was like a man with wings," Mallette told the *Point Pleasant Register* the next day. "It wasn't anything like you'd seen on TV or in a monster movie." It flew with grace at what looked like a high speed. But it was clumsy on foot.

"I'm a hard guy to scare," Scarberry told the paper, "but last night, I was for getting out of there."

Wildlife biologist Dr. Robert L. Smith believed the couples saw a sandhill crane, but the men disagreed. So did dozens of other witnesses who saw the mysterious creature during the next thirteen months.

When the Silver Bridge failed on December 15, 1967, many local West Virginians blamed the Mothman for the deaths of forty-six people lost to the collapse.

In the summer of 2017, the Mothman re-emerged, this time in Chicago, Illinois. John Amitrano was working a Friday night shift at The Owl, a popular Logan Square destination, when he saw something in the sky. "It didn't look like a bat so much as what illustrations of pterodactyls look like," he told VICE News. "I know what birds and what bats look like. This thing didn't have any feathers or fur, and it didn't fly like anything I've ever seen."

Fifty-four other people reported seeing the same thing over Chicago in the months that followed—a human-like figure—and it has Lon Strickler, author of *Mothman Dynasty: Chicago's Winged Humanoids* astonished.

"This group of sightings is historical in cryptozoology terms," Strickler said. "For one, it's happening in an urban area for the most part, and that there are so many sightings in one period."

Is the Chicago Mothman a harbinger of doom? Strickler doubts it. But he doesn't doubt its authenticity. "I think they're flesh-and-blood beings that are not of this world," he said.

Mothman juvenile

NEW JERSEY DEVIL

(new jer-zee DEV-il)

FIRST REPORTED:	**1909**
LOCATION:	**NEW JERSEY, UNITED STATES**
CRYPTID TYPE:	**TERRESTRIAL/AERIAL; BAT-LIKE**
REALITY RATING:	★ ★ ★

FACTOID: In 1982, a National Hockey League team, first known as the Kansas City Scouts, then the Colorado Rockies, moved to New Jersey. Ten thousand eager fans voted on a fresh name for the franchise in June, and the New Jersey Devils name was victorious. The cryptozoological creature from the Pine Barrens in southern New Jersey was the new name's inspiration.

EYEWITNESS ACCOUNT: A horrific curse supposedly brought the New Jersey Devil to life during the 1700s in the Pine Barrens region of New Jersey. A woman named Deborah Smith married Daniel Leeds and became Mother Leeds. She gave birth to twelve healthy children. But the thirteenth was cursed, so Deborah delivered a beast.

New Jersey Devil, a horse with wings

The New Jersey Devil stood on two hooved feet and flew with wings stretched tight on its bones, like those of a bat. Its head was shaped like a goat or a horse, depending on which version of the story you examine. Once the troubled birth was complete, the newborn Jersey Devil reportedly flew around the room, then escaped and disappeared.

When Daniel Leeds died, he named twelve children in his 1736 will. But his last child was disowned.

Random people claimed to have seen the New Jersey Devil throughout New Jersey state history. But Kean University historian Brian Regal says there is a more commonplace reason for the monster tale.

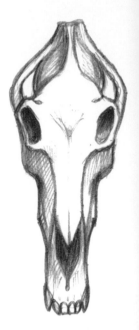

Adult New Jersey Devil skull

Daniel Leeds, a Quaker, decided to publish an almanac to compete with the volumes created by Benjamin Franklin. When Leeds added astrological elements to his almanac, his fellow Quakers turned on him, calling the astrology too "pagan" for the community. The books were censored or destroyed by the town. Leeds resisted and published even more controversial content. The town dubbed him, his wife, and his children "evil." So in a sense, they were the first New Jersey Devils.

Regardless of origins, stories featuring the odd animal continue to unfold. An anonymous construction worker captured a photograph of the New Jersey Devil during a storm in November of 2015, just outside of Philadelphia. He and his friends were driving home when they thought they saw a giant vulture.

They photographed the creature and reviewed the images at home. That's when they realized what they saw was no bird. It was the spitting image of the legendary New Jersey Devil, with bat-like wings and goat-like features. It was nothing like any animal they'd ever seen before. Does the New Jersey Devil still haunt the Jersey skies? It may, at least in the hawk-eyed view of New Jersey's most observant drivers.

New Jersey Devil foal

*Orang Pendek
may be the next
confirmed cryptid*

ORANG PENDEK

(oh-RANG pen-deck)

FIRST REPORTED:	**1818**
LOCATION:	**SUMATRA, INDONESIA**
CRYPTID TYPE:	**TERRESTRIAL; APE-LIKE**
REALITY RATING:	★ ★ ★ ★ ★

FACTOID: Orang Pendek, meaning "short person," may be a rare bipedal ape species living in the wilds of Sumatra. But local experts say it isn't the only one. The Orang Kardil may also roam the thick Asian jungle. Orang Kardil means "tiny men." Roughly three feet tall, the elusive creatures wander naked, hunting with poisoned bamboo spears. When their hunts are unsuccessful, they are known for stealing human food stores.

EYEWITNESS ACCOUNT: It's hard to nail down the first credible sighting of Orang Pendek, the mysterious bipedal ape of the island of Sumatra. Tribal natives, who once called it Sedapa, have always known the creature lurks in the thick jungles of the equatorial rain forest. But they share their stories orally, not in the written word.

Englishman William Marsden filed a brief written report in 1818. But Dr. Edward Jacobson, a Dutch scientist and settler in Sumatra, took a more studied interest in 1910 when Sumatran Governor L. C. Westernek shared a written eyewitness report with him. The estate foreman who wrote the account saw the Orang Pendek, just yards away.

Adult Orang Pendek skull

It was "a large creature, low on its feet, which ran like a man, and was about to cross [my] path. It was very hairy and it was not an orangutan, but its face was not like an ordinary man's. It silently and gravely gave [us] a disagreeable stare, and calmly ran away."

Dr. Jacobson researched the creature. He collected stories, footprints, and other physical evidence for five years, then published a paper in *De Tropische Natuur*, a tropical nature magazine, in 1917.

Cryptozoologists like Adam Davies, expedition leader for the Centre for Fortean Zoology, continue Jacobson's work today. Author Richard Freeman, who wrote *Orang Pendek: Sumatra's Forgotten Ape*, joined the quest for the fourth time in September of 2011.

"On one trek, on the far side of [a] lake—an area with damper, thicker jungle," Freeman wrote in the *Guardian* newspaper, "[we] found a print next to a rotting log that had been ripped apart. Orang pendek have been seen feeding off grubs in such logs. The print was cast [. . .] using quick-drying dental plaster."

Once the cast was cleaned, Freeman got a closer look. "It was clearly a handprint, rather than a footprint," he wrote. "The palm was rounded, the thumb short and almost triangular, and the fingers were thick and sausage-shaped. The structure was quite unlike that of the Sumatran orangutan with its long thin fingers and almost vestigial thumb."

Freeman's party suspects it is more evidence that Orang Pendek is real. And they are not alone.

In February of 2018, Jonathan Downes, director of the Centre for Fortean Zoology, shared a video taken by Sumatrans exploring the countryside via motorcycle. As they flew down a narrow dirt road, something strange came into focus, and they got it on camera. A short, muscular bipedal creature covered in hair ran from the cyclists and ducked into tall grass on the left side of the road.

Baby Orang Pendek

After reviewing the evidence, adding it to evidence he's collected for years, the fifty-nine-year-old cryptozoologist made a bold claim in the United Kingdom's *Daily Star* newspaper: "If I was going to put a probability on the existence of [Orang Pendek], I would say 99 percent."

According to Downes, it's only a matter of time until the scientific world agrees.

PIASA BIRD

(PIE-ah-saw bird)

FIRST REPORTED:	1673
LOCATION:	ILLINOIS, UNITED STATES
CRYPTID TYPE:	AERIAL; BIRD-LIKE
REALITY RATING:	★

FACTOID: In April of 2015, paleontologist Daniel Irving Green claimed to find the fossilized skull of the Piasa Bird in an Alton, Illinois, cave he'd been exploring since he was in second grade. "Today is the greatest day of my life. I feel validated," he told Brittany Kohler, a reporter at Riverbender.com. But no other experts have substantiated his claim.

EYEWITNESS ACCOUNT: Though the original carvings of the Piasa Bird were likely prehistoric in North American terms, one of the earliest written reports of the artwork came from Father Jacques Marquette in 1673.

Marquette joined the Society of Jesus at age seventeen. After working and teaching in France, he was sent as a missionary to work with the indigenous people of America

Piasa Bird is a terrifying legend

in 1666. His personal records are plentiful. He wrote about the bird while exploring the Mississippi River Valley.

While wondering at rock formations that towered far above the river banks, Marquette spotted two painted monsters feared and forbidden by local tribes. "They are as large as a calf," Marquette wrote about the painting. "They have horns on their heads like those of a deer, a horrible look, red eyes, a beard like a tiger's, a face somewhat like a man's, a body covered with scales, and so long a tail that it winds all around the body, passing above the head and going back between the legs, ending in a fish's tail."

Adult Piasa Bird skull

Tones of green, red, and black brought the reliefs to life. John Russell, a professor of Greek and Latin at Shurtleff College in Alton, Illinois, named the creature the Piasa Bird—the bird that devours men—in 1836. Russell claimed the animal had once thrived in the cliffs, feeding on Native American people downstream.

Illini Chief Ouatoga was said to have lured the monster into an open space. When it caught the chief in its talons, Ouatoga clung to the roots of an ancient tree. His kinsmen shot a series of poisonous arrows into the giant bird's flesh, ending its life. The art was carved in historic tribute.

Russell eventually admitted his tale was imaginary—
a fact Dr. Duane Esarey of the Illinois State Archaeological
Survey confirmed with extensive research. But the historic
image remained popular. In the late 1870s, the Mississippi
Lime Company started mining the limestone cliff, and the
Piasa Bird image was quarried away. It was repainted based
on hand-drawn copies of the original artwork on a new,
less stable location near Alton, Illinois. It continues to be
repainted when it fades away.

Piasa Bird juvenile imagined

Piltdown Man: the missing link?

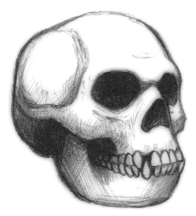

Adult human skull

Adult gorilla skull

PILTDOWN MAN

(PILT-down man)

FIRST REPORTED:	1912
LOCATION:	EAST SUSSEX, ENGLAND
CRYPTID TYPE:	TERRESTRIAL; HUMANOID-LIKE
REALITY RATING:	★

FACTOID: The Piltdown Man wasn't Charles Dawson's only false claim. The amateur fossil hunter was responsible for at least thirty-eight fake finds, according to the *Telegraph* newspaper in Great Britain. Experts believe Dawson hoped to achieve scientific glory. Instead, he's remembered as a grade-A fraud.

EYEWITNESS ACCOUNT: The Piltdown Man was a so-called missing link between modern man, called *Homo sapiens* by scientists, and their prehistoric ancestors, called hominids. The discovery was revealed on December 18, 1912, by British paleontologist Arthur Smith Woodward.

Heralded around the world, the fossil puzzle pieces—five skull fragments, a lower jaw with two teeth, and an isolated canine tooth—were thought to prove that apes and men were even more closely linked than had been previously believed. And Charles Dawson was the star of the show.

Dawson was allegedly given the bulk of the fossils by a mysterious man digging in a gravel pit in Piltdown.

When he went back to prospect in the same locale in 1911, he unearthed more skull fragments and stone tools and readily shared the whole collection with Woodward.

Astonished by the human-like skull fragments and the ape-like jaw, Woodward proudly proclaimed the find *Eoanthropus dawsoni*—Dawson's Dawn Man. It was the only hominid ever discovered in Great Britain—except it wasn't a hominid at all.

Modern scientists eventually used new technology to more accurately define the strange jumble of bones and made a startling discovery. The skull fragments appeared humanoid because they were. They were most likely pieces of a contemporary human skull or skulls. And the jaw looked ape-like because it belonged to a modern orangutan.

Dawson apparently took special care to cover his tracks, at least in terms of early-twentieth-century techniques. He packed the jaw with tiny pebbles beneath the teeth to give the fossil heft. Fossils are heavier than actual bone. He used putty to smooth the fit of the fabricated skull replica. And he stained all the pieces to make them look like authentic ancient finds.

All signs pointed to Dawson, though he died before his hoax was discovered, so he could never be questioned about his deception. But the conclusion is near unanimous: the Piltdown Man was a hoax and a reminder to wait for the facts before drawing scientific conclusions you might regret.

The International Museum of Cryptozoology

4 Thompson's Point Road, #106
Portland, Maine 04102 | CryptozoologyMuseum.com

Loren Coleman may be the best known cryptozoologist in the world. For decades, he's investigated mysterious claims of creatures worldwide. With a critical eye, he's rejected hoaxes and documented thousands of credible stories in books and television documentaries.

His extensive travels have helped him curate a collection of more than ten thousand artifacts that capture the spirit and focus of cryptozoology—the study of animals that may or may not be real. And those artifacts are on display in the International Museum of Cryptozoology in Portland, Maine.

Prior to securing a storefront location, the treasures were carefully stored at Coleman's private residence, where only a select few (including the author of this book) could tour the wonders of his life's work. Today, the general public can explore the collection every day—winter, spring, summer, or fall—excluding Tuesdays.

What inspired this unusual vocation? According to an interview in the *Los Angeles Times*, Coleman credits a screening of *Half Human*, a film about the infamous Abominable Snowman—and his keen sense of curiosity.

"I'm an open-minded skeptic and I'm skeptically open-minded," he says. "[I] support critical thinking."

PUKWUDGIE

(PUCK-wuh-gee)

FIRST REPORTED:	UNKNOWN
LOCATION:	NEW ENGLAND, UNITED STATES
CRYPTID TYPE:	TERRESTRIAL; TROLL-LIKE
REALITY RATING:	★ ★

FACTOID: Harry Potter author J. K. Rowling created another wizarding school for her Fantastic Beasts and Where to Find Them movie series: American students went to Ilvermorny, not Hogwarts. And one of the houses they might have been sorted into was called Pukwudgie. It's likely that Ms. Rowling was inspired by this cryptid.

EYEWITNESS ACCOUNT: When the Wampanoag and other East Coast tribal people made their home in what would eventually be called New England, they told the tales of tricksters with magical powers. The Pukwudgie—meaning people of the wilderness—were just such tricksters.

Barely three feet tall, the troll-like creatures with oversized ears, hands, and facial features had grayish skin.

kwudgie was a trickster

At first, they were not a danger. They were full of mischief, but not evil. But they became more and more difficult.

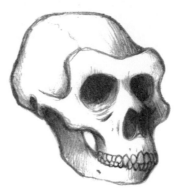

Adult Pukwudgie skull

The Wampanoag asked a loving, god-like giant called Maushop and his wife Granny Squanit to punish the Pukwudgie. They shook them and scattered them across New England in banishment.

When the Pukwudgie returned, they did so with a vengeance, demanding blood and creating mayhem. Not only were they fierce; their magical powers made them hard to contain. They could vanish at will or transform into other animal shapes. They used poisonous weapons in battle, and were able to produce fire from thin air. Plus, they could control the soul of any human being they killed.

Maushop and Granny Squanit went to war against the Pukwudgie, killing as many as they could. The Pukwudgie disappeared until Maushop and Granny Squanit faded away. Those that remain are said to cause trouble even today.

Baby Pukwudgie

Ropen, the pterosaur of Papua New Guinea

ROPEN

(ROPE-in)

FIRST REPORTED:	1935
LOCATION:	BOUGAINVILLE ISLAND, PAPUA NEW GUINEA
CRYPTID TYPE:	AERIAL; PTEROSAUR-LIKE
REALITY RATING:	★ ★

FACTOID: The Ropen could be part of New Guinea native people's ancient mythology. Wood and stone carvings of the Wokam birdman, a prehistoric god, feature a crested head atop a humanoid body, very much like the legend of the Ropen.

EYEWITNESS ACCOUNT: Most stories of the Ropen suggest it is a giant flying predator in Papua New Guinea—a nocturnal hunter the local people call the "Demon Flyer." Credible eyewitness reports are hard to find, but most Ropen enthusiasts think it's a super-size bat, a gigantic bird, or a prehistoric throwback—a pterosaur, complete with bony crested head and a long, pointed tail.

The nocturnal hunter is said to have bioluminescence to lure fish to the water's surface in the dark. But flight instructor Duane Hodgkinson saw one in broad daylight. He was stationed in Papua New Guinea during World War II in 1944. A local guide led Hodgkinson and his team to a grassy clearing where they heard a thrashing in the brush.

They looked and saw what Hodgkinson, in a 2005 interview, first described as a bird taking off. "It was huge," he said. The grass below rustled under the power of the creature's wing flaps. When it circled and flew past, Hodgkinson said he got a perfect side view. "It had [a] long appendage out of the back of its head," he said, "a long neck, and [. . .] it was a dark color."

Hodgkinson later compared the "bird" he saw to a creature in the comic strip *Alley Oop*—a pterodactyl. At one time, Hodgkinson owned a small airplane, a Piper Tri-Pacer with a twenty-nine-foot wingspan. He said the creature had a similar wingspan.

Hodgkinson died in September of 2014 in his hometown of Livingston, Montana, without recanting his story. But more recent witnesses support his claim, thousands of miles from Papua New Guinea—in the United States.

In 2015, an unknown resident of Idaho, posted a video on YouTube that appears to be a

Adult Ropen skull

pterosaur. No further details were included.

Idaho Museum of Natural History director Dr. Leif Tapanila is highly skeptical. "Everyone loves monsters," he told the *Idaho State Journal* newspaper, "and a giant flying reptile sure would be cool to see for real. *Jurassic World* was a massive success because people are excited to imagine how we might interact with these amazing beasts."

Ropen hatchling

It would be cool, but Dr. Tapanila thinks anyone with basic computer skills could fake a prehistoric flyer. In fact, he says, "this video made me laugh out loud. The internet is full of outlandish videos."

Smithsonian Magazine journalist Brian Switek believes such sightings are misidentifications. "Some might be disappointed that there is no evidence of living pterosaurs," he wrote, "but there is another way to look at [it]." The frigatebird in the video is remarkable, too.

"It is a living, flying dinosaur," Switek says, "a modified descendant of small, feathered theropod dinosaur which lived many millions of years ago. To me, that fact is even more wonderful than the discovery of any long-lost species."

SNALLYGASTER

(snal-ee-GAS-ter)

FIRST REPORTED:	1730s
LOCATION:	MARYLAND, UNITED STATES
CRYPTID TYPE:	AERIAL; DRAGON-LIKE
REALITY RATING:	★ ★

FACTOID: Snallygaster is actually the mispronunciation of a German term—*Schneller Geist*—which means "quick spirit." The gentle ghosts were originally blamed for knocking trinkets off tables, not for gobbling up livestock.

EYEWITNESS ACCOUNT: For decades, German settlers in Frederick County, Maryland, passed down stories of the Snallygaster—a beast that stole livestock by soaring down from the sky to pluck them out of the pastures and corrals.

Those impacted by the feathered, dragon-like creature in the 1730s began to post hex symbols on the outer walls of their barns and outbuildings to ward off the monstrous thieves. But considering the dragon's ferocity, painted symbols were flimsy barriers.

A German dragon to fear

According to legends, the Snallygaster commanded thunderous explosions and screeched with a mind-bending pitch. Razor-sharp beaks and talons snatched men and animals with ease, often leaving their bodies drained of blood and scorched in the countryside.

Reporters from local newspapers covered the attacks, warning strangers to avoid the dangerous mountain region. Rumors spread that *National Geographic* was mounting an expedition to catch or photograph the beast.

As panic set in, a new rumor was floated. The monster was dead, drowned in a vat of whiskey mash on a Baltimore County farm. But when Federal officials came to examine the body, the illegal still exploded, taking the Snallygaster's remains with it.

Adult Snallygaster skull

At the time, people believed the dragon was a true monster, terrorizing the communities. But today, there are those who believe the creature was invented to discourage strangers from hiking the woods where stills were hidden during Prohibition, a time when alcoholic drinks were illegal.

If the stills stayed hidden, the moonshiners stayed out of jail. So the Snallygaster was a convenient monster to have around.

Snallygaster hatchling

Thetis Lake Monster, a true classic

THETIS LAKE MONSTER

(THEE-tis Lake Monster)

FIRST REPORTED:	1972
LOCATION:	BRITISH COLUMBIA, CANADA
CRYPTID TYPE:	AQUATIC; HUMANOID-LIKE
REALITY RATING:	★ ★

FACTOID: *The Creature from the Black Lagoon* was one of the last 1950s monster movies made with old-school 3D film technology. Picture paper 3D glasses with one red lens and one blue—very different from the glasses we use today. Gill-man, the film's aquatic star, was a fictional prehistoric monster from the Amazon rain forest in South America. It looked very much like eyewitness descriptions of the Thetis Lake Monster. Is art reflecting true life? Or did the movie influence the eyewitnesses? We may never know.

EYEWITNESS ACCOUNT: For nearly twenty years, Gill-man was considered pure fiction. Then two teenagers claimed to have been attacked by its cousin in British Columbia, Canada. According to the *Victoria Daily Times*, the boys were chased from the Thetis Lake beach in 1972 by a silver, scale-covered biped five feet tall. One of the boys had a bloody wound left "by six razor-sharp points on the monster's head."

Police said the boys "[seemed] sincere, and until we [determined] otherwise, we [had] no alternative but to continue our investigation." Four days later, a man reported his pet tegu lizard missing near the lake. It was three feet long with black-and-white skin. Satisfied the boys had actually seen the aggressive lizard, law enforcement closed the case.

Daniel Loxton, editor of the *Junior Skeptic* magazine in Victoria, never believed the tegu lizard explanation.

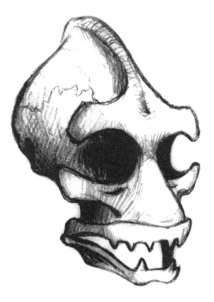

Adult Thetis Lake Monster skull

Thetis Lake Monster juvenile

But he didn't believe the eyewitness story, either. In 2009, he checked the 1972 television listings on a hunch, and his suspicions were confirmed. About a week before the "attack," a local station had played *Beach Girls and the Monster*, a movie about an aquatic monster attacking teenagers.

The two witnesses later admitted their story was a hoax, but the legend lingered. In 2012, fishermen said they saw the "lizard man" on the lake, and another eyewitness saw a humanoid with webbed hands and a monster face eating cat food on the back porch of a nearby house. Some stories don't die as easily as Gill-man.

THYLACINE

(THY-lah-ceen)

FIRST REDISCOVERED:	**1973**
LOCATION:	**ACROSS AUSTRALIA, VARIOUS**
CRYPTID TYPE:	**TERRESTRIAL; DOG-LIKE**
REALITY RATING:	★ ★ ★ ★ ★

FACTOID: The Beaumaris Zoo in Tasmania started caging thylacines, also called Tasmanian tigers, in 1908. They hosted the last-known living thylacine, sometimes called "Benjamin," until it died in 1936, cold and alone.

EYEWITNESS ACCOUNT: Thylacines are not creatures of our imaginations, not really. They are marsupial wonders driven extinct by man and dogs who misunderstood their place in

Did the thylacine really go extinct?

the ecological system of Australia and Tasmania. The last of the population was slaughtered in Tasmania, less than a hundred years ago.

Australian aboriginal hunters knew better. In prehistoric days, they honored the dog-like animals and captured their likenesses on painted rocks before they went extinct on the continent three thousand years ago. More than five thousand paintings in Australia's Northern Territory still remind the living of the dead.

But are they really gone? Did the last sixty-pound thylacine really perish in 1936, less than a century ago?

Adult Thylacine skull

Perhaps. But there are scientists trying to bring the species back through genetic modification. "One of the things we were interested in was how come they look so much like dogs, even though they are so distantly related?" said Andrew Pask, a biologist at the University of Melbourne, in the *New York Times*. He sequenced the thylacine genome in 2017 and suspects dogs and thylacine experienced convergent evolution—they evolved to look alike because they filled a similar niche in their habitats.

Pask and other scientists hope to bring the thylacine back from extinction, and the science is state of the art. But there are eagle-eyed observers who think a scattered few thylacine may have escaped the devastation.

Many people have captured video of alleged thylacines in the past fifty years, including an anonymous woman from southwest Victoria who captured convincing video of what looks like a thylacine limping across an open field in 2008.

She had seen others, when she was without a camera, more than a dozen times before.

But when Greg Booth and his father, Joe, unveiled their video in 2017, local experts took notice. "I didn't believe [it]," Booth, a logger and wood cutter from the Central Highlands said in a Fox News interview. "But when it's in front of you, now I have no doubt at all."

Booth first shared his evidence with Adrian "Richo" Richardson, a man who has been researching thylacines for more than twenty-five years. "I don't think it's a thylacine," he said, "I know it's a thylacine." So they joined forces to collect more evidence and present it at a press conference.

Regional wildlife biologist Nick Mooney reviewed the images and said, "Assuming the footage is authentic, the animal is either a very large spotted-tail quoll or a small thylacine." He gives Booth and Richardson a one-in-three chance of being correct.

Their findings have been forwarded to the Tasmanian government in hopes they will consider protecting the small population that may still live and breed in the outback.

Thylacine pup

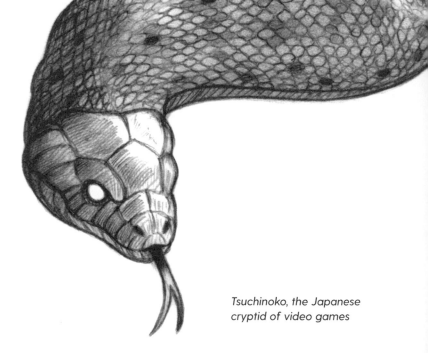

Tsuchinoko, the Japanese cryptid of video games

TSUCHINOKO

(TSUCH-ee-no-koh)

FIRST RECORDED:	700 CE
LOCATION:	JAPAN: VARIOUS LOCATIONS
CRYPTID TYPE:	TERRESTRIAL; SNAKE-LIKE
REALITY RATING:	★ ★ ★

FACTOID: Finding a living Tsuchinoko may be all but impossible, but thanks to Clawmark Toys, you can buy a resin replica. "Each [. . .] figure is polyvinyl resin," the ad says, "and beautifully detailed." But the figures are out of production, so don't wait too long to add them to your collection.

EYEWITNESS ACCOUNT: First documented in eighth-century Japanese mythology, the Tsuchinoko is allegedly a legless, snake-like creature one foot to two and a half feet long. It had a snake-like head, a fat body and a thin tail.

Considered venomous, it has the fangs of a viper, but what is really frightening is its supposed ability to leap a great distance in pursuit of its prey—or in defense of its territory.

Ancient legends suggested the Tsuchinoko could speak and was prone to dishonesty. Other stories said it chirped like a high-pitched bird.

Adult Tsuchinoko skull

For almost five hundred years, the Japanese have searched for the fabled creature, sometimes for monetary gains. In the year 2000, the local government in Yoshii, Okayama, offered ¥20 million—nearly $200,000—as reward for proof the Tsuchinoko might be real.

The odds of finding proof are slim, but finding Tsuchinoko fans is much easier. This odd reptile showed up in multiple *Metal Gear Solid* video games, and *Pokémon*'s character Dunsparce is allegedly based on the Tsuchinoko. A character in the *Yo-kai Watch* game and anime series is also Tsuchinoko-inspired. The memes took flight on Tumblr and Twitter as #TsuchinokoReal.

Tsuchinoko hatchling

Big Money Reward for Nessie and Friends

Jon Downes, the director of the Centre for Fortean Zoology, does not believe in the Loch Ness Monster. But he helped launch a £50,000 (more than $64,000) bounty in the United Kingdom for proof that he's wrong.

In January of 2018, Downes temporarily joined the Capcom team to help promote their video game, *Monster Hunter: World*, with a friendly competition—a stack of cash for anyone who could prove one of ten cryptid monsters might actually be real.

"When planning the upcoming launch of *Monster Hunter: World*, we couldn't help but keep coming back to the real-life monsters we've all heard stories about since we were kids," said Capcom's senior public relations manager, Laura Skelly. "Speaking to the world's leading real-life monster hunter, Jon Downes, we were inspired to reopen investigations."

Which ten creatures were on the list? Bigfoot, the Loch Ness Monster, the Mongolian Death Worm, the Mermaid, the Earth Hound, the Yeti, the Chupacabra, the Flying Snake of Nambia, the Yowie, and the Cornish Owlman.

The deadline for proof was June of 2018. Did some lucky British cryptozoologist take home the prize? Sadly, the treasure went unclaimed. But better luck next time.

VEO

(VEE-oh)

FIRST REPORTED:	**1926**
LOCATION:	**RINTJA, INDONESIA**
CRYPTID TYPE:	**TERRESTRIAL; PANGOLIN-LIKE**
REALITY RATING:	★ ★

FACTOID: Validating the existence of the Veo, a giant armored pangolin, may not be easy today. Its ancient ancestor, *Manis paleojavanicus*, lived in Malaysia until it went extinct thousands of years ago.

EYEWITNESS ACCOUNT: Eight kinds of modern pangolins are endangered species due to overhunting in their natural habitats in Africa and Asia. Poachers sell the animals as luxury meat or for body parts thought to have medicinal properties. Such medicinal properties do not exist, however, so the slaughter is misguided.

Even so, pangolins have lived for thousands of years. And cryptozoologists believe a giant pangolin called the Veo may still live on the islands of Java and Borneo.

Veo, the giant pangolin

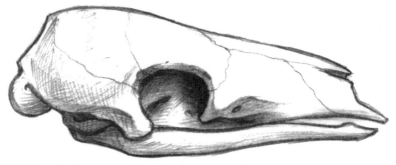

Adult Veo skull

The unconfirmed pangolin species is thought to be the size of a small horse—up to twelve feet long. It is a nocturnal mountain dweller and an insectivore that lives on a diet of ants and termites.

In his book *The Beasts that Hide from Man: Seeking the World's Last Undiscovered Animals*, Karl Shuker writes that the Veo lives on the southeast island of Rintja. He groups the Veo with *Stegosaurus, Ankylosaurus,* and other armored dinosaurs because, like its smaller modern counterpart, it is covered in protective plates. If this cryptid turns out to be real, it may be a rare population of the prehistoric *Manis paleojavanicus* that escaped extinction. But very little physical evidence suggests the population really exists.

A living Veo would have giant claws meant for self-defense and for breaking into termite mounds. Where modern pangolins curl up in a ball when threatened, the Veo would probably use its size, whip-like tail, and sharp claws for protection. It would likely weigh a ton, if it's ever confirmed as real.

Veo juvenile

*Wolfman sightings
are on the rise*

WOLFMAN OF CHESTNUT MOUNTAIN

(WOLF-man of CHESS-nut mown-tain)

FIRST REPORTED:	2010
LOCATION:	ILLINOIS, UNITED STATES
CRYPTID TYPE:	TERRESTRIAL; DOG-LIKE
REALITY RATING:	★ ★

FACTOID: According to author Carol Rose, the history of werewolves is as ancient as we are. In her book, *Giants, Monsters, and Dragons*, Rose said, "In ancient Greece it was believed that a person could be transformed by eating the meat of a wolf that had been mixed with [the meat] of a human." According to Greek mythology, the condition was permanent.

EYEWITNESS ACCOUNT: The transformation of human into wolf is known as lycanthropy. And author Linda S. Godfrey has spent decades studying eyewitness accounts of human interactions with lycanthropic monsters "bigger than they ought to be," she says.

One such story was featured in her book, *American Monsters: A History of Monster Lore, Legends, and Sightings in America.*

According to Godfrey, behavioral psychologist Rachel Gendreau and her fiancé were driving through the thick woods of Galena, Illinois, about twenty miles from Dubuque, Iowa, in 2010. By the light of a full moon, they witnessed the impossible—a wolfman.

"I prefer 'unknown upright canine,'" Godfrey says.

As they neared Chestnut Mountain, the couple saw the creature standing upright on its hind legs, white eyes gleaming. They moved forward, but after a brief look at the couple, it bounded into the woods at breakneck speed.

"What [. . .] was that? Did you see it?" Gendreau asked her fiancé, according to Godfrey.

"I don't know what it was," her fiancé answered, "but it had dog legs."

When Gendreau caught her breath, she looked in the rearview mirror, and there it was again. The creature had circled back and was gazing at the car. Terrified, the couple sped away, still uncertain of what they'd seen.

Adult Wolfman skull

Wolfman pup

According to Godfrey, they'd come face to face with the Wolfman of Chestnut Mountain, an animal legendary in the region for years. Such experiences are rare, the author admits, but not unheard of.

"I think there are more sightings," she says, "but people don't want to be ridiculed. Some are in denial. They don't want to admit what they see."

YETI

(YEH-tee)

FIRST REPORTED:	**1800s**
LOCATION:	**HIMALAYAS, NEPAL**
CRYPTID TYPE:	**TERRESTRIAL; APE-LIKE**
REALITY RATING:	★ ★ ★ ★ ★

FACTOID: A gigantic ape once dominated the wilderness of Asia—and it did so for six to nine million years. *Gigantopithecus*, the hulking 1,200-pound, ten-foot-tall primate, would have dwarfed all known great apes on record today. Most experts believe *Gigantopithecus* went extinct one hundred thousand years ago, but did it? Or did it evolve to become the infamous Yeti of the Himalayas? It's a question some anthropologists are beginning to take seriously, but it has not yet been fully answered.

EYEWITNESS ACCOUNT: For centuries, the people indigenous to Nepal, Bhutan, and Tibet (China) have believed in a mysterious biped—a giant ape Western culture has called the Yeti. Tibetan sherpa Dawa was happy to share his grandfather's explanation of what the creature looked like.

Yeti, the bigfoot of the Himalayas

In *Hunt for the Abominable Snowman,* a *National Geographic* documentary, Dawa explained, "Back in 1961, my grandfather went to the [. . .] Harlem Zoo. When he saw the gorilla, he got really excited and he said, 'That's a yeti, it's a yeti.' Years later, people would come to him with pictures of a bear, [. . .] and he would say, 'I know what a bear is, but that's not a yeti. A yeti is like this,' and he would point specifically to a picture of a gorilla."

Adult Yeti skull

Author Daniel Taylor sides with the bear camp in his book, *Yeti, the Ecology of a Mystery.* And he went to Barun, one of the most untamed jungles of the region, to prove it. "I was advised to go there by the King of Nepal," Taylor said in an interview. "And when the king says that, you go, because he really knows his country."

Almost immediately, he found footprints. "I'd seen footprints before," he said, "but these were fresh. And I had no doubt I had found the Yeti." What he did doubt was what a Yeti actually was. He concluded the tracks, and likely all Yeti tracks, were left by a black bear that locals considered a "tree bear." By using its fifth claw like an opposable thumb, it had become adept at scaling trees.

Some samples of hair, scat, and bone support Taylor's belief. Nine specimens were collected as possible Yeti artifacts. Eight were confirmed as being from bears via DNA analysis—the ninth was dog. These samples do disprove the primate theory. But others do not.

Professor Bryan Sykes of the University of Oxford had fifty different hair strands analyzed, also thought to be from the Yeti. Twenty-eight were confirmed as hairs from various bears. But two were impossible to identify as known animals, leaving the possibility of an unknown Yeti on the scientific table.

Dawa knows bear species inhabit the mountains of Asia. But like his grandfather, and thousands of other people living in the Himalayas, he insists Yetis do too—Yetis related to great apes, feeding on meat, fruits, and vegetables, just as the people do. He says the Yeti is not white, as is often depicted in Western fiction. It is brown or reddish brown but covered in snow during the harshest winter months.

Which camp is correct? It's impossible to say. Evidence and evidence alone will settle the friendly dispute.

Yeti toddler

Appendices

Cryptid Types around the World

Hundreds of cryptid stories are told all over the world. Some of the animals reported are unique. But many are similar animals sighted all over the globe. These lists represent a few "types" of cryptids and the names by which they're known on many continents. Those profiled in this book are marked in bold print, in case you'd like to go back and read more. But don't be afraid to do research of your own. New stories are popping up regularly. Doing your own search for evidence could expand what we know about these mysterious creatures.

BIPEDAL APE-LIKE CRYPTIDS

AGOGWE—Africa

ALMASTY—Russia

BIGFOOT—nickname for all North American bipedal ape sightings

FOUKE MONSTER—Arkansas (USA)

GRASSMAN—Ohio (USA)

HAIRY MAN—Native American (USA)

HIBAGON—Japan

MURPHYSBORO MUDDY MONSTER (ALBINO)—Illinois (USA)

ORANG PENDEK—Sumatra

SASQUATCH—Pacific Northwest (USA)

SKUNK APE—Florida (USA)

WENDIGO—Canada

YEREN—China

YETI—Himalayas

YOWIE—Australia

WATER MONSTERS

ALTAMAHA-HA—Georgia (USA)

CHAMP—Vermont/New York (USA)

KAPPA—Japan

LAKE TIANCHI MONSTER—China

LAKE VAN MONSTER—Turkey

LOCH NESS MONSTER—Scotland

MORGAWR—Great Britain

MUSSIE—Canada

OGOPOGO—Canada

QALUPALIK—Alaska (USA)

SELMA—Norway

TAHOE TESSIE—California (USA)

THETIS LAKE MONSTER—Canada

YACUMAMA—South America

ZIN—West Africa

DINOSAUR/LIZARD CRYPTIDS

BEAST OF BUSCO—Indiana

BROSNO DRAGON—Russia

BURU—India

EMELA-NTOUKA—Central Africa

KONGAMATO—Zambia

KUMI LIZARD—New Zealand

MAHAMBA—Republic of the Congo

MBIELU-MBIELU-MBIELU—Republic of the Congo

MOKELE-MBEMBE—Republic of the Congo

MUHURU—Kenya

MURRAY—Papua New Guinea

NAGAS—India

NGOUBOU—Cameroon

NGUMA-MONENE—Republic of the Congo

SHARLIE—Idaho (USA)

HUMANOID CRYPTIDS

DOVER DEMON—Massachusetts (USA)

ENFIELD HORROR—Illinois (USA)

FRESNO NIGHTCRAWLERS—California (USA)

GOATMAN—Maryland (USA)

GRAY—Global

KELLY-HOPKINSVILLE GOBLIN—Kentucky (USA)

LIZARD MAN OF SCAPE ORE SWAMP—South Carolina (USA)

MAN BAT—Mississippi (USA)

MELON HEADS—Connecticut (USA)

MHUWE—Delaware (USA)

MENEHUNE—Hawaii (USA)

QALUPALIK—Alaska (USA)

PUKWUDGIE—New England (USA)

ROUGAROU—Louisiana (USA)

WOLFMAN OF CHESTNUT MOUNTAIN—Illinois (USA)

SNAKE/WORM CRYPTIDS

ARABHAR—Middle East

CROWING CRESTED COBRA—Africa

GIANT ANACONDA—South America

GIANT CONGO SNAKE—Republic of the Congo

GIANT WORM OF THE MOJAVE—California (USA)

GROOTSLANG—South Africa

HOOP SNAKE—Wisconsin (USA)

LAGARFLJÓT WORM—Iceland

LAMBTON WORM—United Kingdom

MINHOCÃO—South America

MONGOLIAN DEATH WORM—China

NABAU—Borneo

NAMIBIAN FLYING SNAKE—Namibia

TATZELWURM—Europe

TSUCHINOKO—Japan

FLYING CRYPTIDS

AHOOL—Indonesia

CRAWFORDSVILLE
MONSTER—Indiana (USA)

FLATWOODS MONSTER—
West Virginia (USA)

FLYING MANTA RAY—West
Virginia (USA)

MOTHMAN—West Virginia
(USA)

NEW JERSEY DEVIL—New
Jersey (USA)

OWLMAN—United Kingdom

POPOBAWA—Tanzania

POUAKAI—Maori

ROPEN—Papau New Guinea

SKYFISH—Global

SNALLYGASTER—Germany/
USA

THUNDERBIRD—Canada/
Alaska

ULAMA/DEVIL BIRD—Sri
Lanka

WAKWAK—Philippines

Read More About It

"A 3-D Look inside the Tasmanian Tiger's Pouch, Long After Extinction."
by Nicholas St. Fleur | NYTimes.com, February 2018

American Monsters: A History of Monster Lore, Legends, and Sightings in America
by Linda S. Godfrey | TarcherPerigee, 2014

Beasts That Hide from Man: Seeking the World's Last Undiscovered Animals
by Karl P. N. Shuker | Paraview Press, 2003

Bigfoot Book: The Encyclopedia of Sasquatch, Yeti, and Cryptid Primates
by Nick Redfern | Visible Ink Press, 2015

Cryptozoology A to Z: The Encyclopedia of Loch Monsters, Sasquatch, Chupacabras, and Other Authentic Mysteries of Nature
by Loren Coleman and Jerome Clark | Simon & Schuster, 1999

"Fantastically Wrong: The Legend of the Kraken, a Monster That Hunts with Its Own Poop."
by Matt Simon | Wired.com, September 2014

"Giant Flesh-Eating Koala of Legend Was Real."
by Brian Switek | NationalGeographic.com, March 2017

Giants, Monsters, and Dragons: An Encyclopedia of Folklore, Legend, and Myth
by Carol Rose | W. W. Norton & Company, 2001

**"How to Solve Human Evolution's
Greatest Hoax."**
by Erin Wayman | Smithsonian.com, December 2012

*Hunting Monsters: Cryptozoology and the
Reality behind the Myths*
by Darren Naish | Sirius, 2017

In Search of Sasquatch
by Kelly Milner Halls | Houghton Mifflin Harcourt, 2011

*Monsters Among Us: An Exploration of Otherworldly Bigfoots,
Wolfmen, Portals, Phantoms, and Odd Phenomena*
by Linda S. Godfrey | TarcherPerigee, 2016

Mothman: Evil Incarnate
by Loren Coleman and Michael D. Winkle | Cosimo Books, 2017

*Still in Search of Prehistoric Survivors:
The Creatures That Time Forgot?*
by Karl P. N. Shuker | Coachwhip Publications, 2016

*Tales of the Cryptids: Mysterious Creatures
That May or May Not Exist*
by Kelly Milner Halls, Rick Spears, and Roxyanne Young |
Millbrook, 2006

"This Man Searched for the Yeti for 60 Years—and Found It."
by Simon Worrall | NationalGeographic.com, August 2017

**"United Monsters of America: Infographic Reveals
the Strange Beasts that Have Captured the Nation's
Imagination."**
by Elli Zolfagharifard | DailyMail.co.uk, January 2015

Glossary

3D FILM [3D film]—movies technically engineered to appear three-dimensional with the use of special glasses. Early 3D required glasses with one red lens and one blue lens to filter out red and blue shading effects. Modern 3D glasses are more effective and not dependent on colored lenses.

ANTHROPOLOGIST [an-thruh-POL-uh-jist]—a scientist who studies the physical, cultural, biological, and social practices of human beings.

BEHEMOTH [bih-HEE-muhth]—any creature or object of enormous size or power.

BLIND-BOX [BLAHYND-boks]—a package designed to block knowledge of what is inside.

CARCASS [KAHR-kuhs]—an animal's dead body.

CEPHALOPODS [SEF-uh-luh-podz]—animals within the class Cephalopoda, including octopus, cuttlefish, and squid.

CRYPTOZOOLOGY [KRIP-toh-zoh-OL-uh-jee]—the study of evidence meant to confirm the existence of animals not yet scientifically confirmed or named.

DISTENDED [dih-STEN-did]—increased in size and volume by internal pressure.

DNA [D-N-A]—an abbreviation for deoxyribonucleic acid, the material that carries the genetic information for all life forms.

ENDOWED [en-DOWD]—provided with talent, physical, or monetary abundance.

EUCALYPTUS [yoo-kuh-LIP-tuhs]—trees native to Australia and surrounding islands.

HOMINIDS [HOM-uh-nidz]—any member of the animal group including modern and extinct humans and great apes.

ISOPODS [AHY-suh-podz]—freshwater, marine, or terrestrial crustaceans with seven pairs of legs.

MARSUPIALS [MAR-soop-ee-alz]—mammals born incompletely developed and transferred to pouches where they drink their mother's milk and finish growing.

NATURALIST [NACH-er-ah-list]—a person who studies natural history.

PETRIFIED [PE-truh-fahyd]—made rigid, as of stone.

PRANK [prangk]—a trick of an amusing or malicious nature.

QUOLL [kwol]—a spotted, cat-like marsupial from Australia and New Guinea.

SATYR [SAY-ter]—a mythological woodland creature, half human and half goat or horse.

SEVERED [SEV-urd]—forcibly divided in part.

STILL [stil]—an apparatus to distill liquids over heat to make alcoholic beverages.

UNDULATING [UHN-juh-leyt-ing]—to move with a wavelike motion.

VULNERABLE [VUHL-ner-uh-buhl]—susceptible to being hurt or wounded.

Index

About the Author

KELLY MILNER HALLS has researched all things weird and wonderful for more than twenty-five years, which means she's old, but young at heart. Her nonfiction books explore modern animals, dinosaurs, mummies, aliens, ghosts, cryptids, and other fascinating subjects. She lives in Spokane, Washington, with two daughters, a Great Dane, and too many cats. Read more about her at WondersofWeird.com.

About the Illustrator

RICK SPEARS was fascinated by dinosaurs as a young child and spent hours drawing prehistoric animal combat scenes. These days, his illustrations can be found in books, magazines, and even a dinosaur board game. His sculptures, including a life-size model of the cryptid sea creature "Altie" (page 14), can be visited in museums. Rick lives in Georgia with his wife, Darlene, and their two pups, Khari and Dante. *Cryptid Creatures* is his third book about the strange world of cryptozoology.